Penn's Woods

Willowcreek Valley Farm Series #4

Trailblazing in Penn's Woods

Carrie Bender

Masthof Press
219 Mill Road
Morgantown, PA 19543-9516

TRAILBLAZING IN PENN'S WOODS

Copyright © 2005

Artwork
by Julie Stauffer Martin, Ephrata, Pa.

* * * * * *

This story is fiction
although it is based on a number of accurate
historical events, especially in regards
to the Herr family at the Hans Herr House
located in Lancaster County, Pennsylvania.

* * * * * *

Library of Congress Control Number: 2005928869
International Standard Book Number: 1-932864-24-5

Published 2005
Masthof Press
219 Mill Road
Morgantown, PA 19543-9516

Contents

1

Voyage to America

Susie Petersheim poured hot melted butter over the bowl of freshly popped popcorn, then liberally sprinkled salt over it and set it on the stand beside the rocker.

Just then Dannie came clumping up the cellar steps with a bowl full of big red apples. "Listen to that wind howling down the chimney," he exclaimed. "I'm awfully glad the temperatures are in the thirties instead of only in the teens or lower. I wouldn't relish having frozen pipes to contend with while I'm responsible for the barn and the animals."

"I'm glad the chores are all done for tonight," Susie said as she selected a juicy red apple, "because that box of books Vernie's sister Savilla sent over have been tantalizing me all evening."

"Me too." Dannie got a soup bowl out of the cupboard and filled it with buttered popcorn. "Steven told me there's not much to do here at Willowcreek Valley Farm, besides tending the stock and chopping firewood to keep the furnace going. There are some Lewis B. Miller books in the box that I haven't read yet. He's my favorite author. I hope to get at least one of them read before Steven, Annie, and little Suzanne come back from their trip to Ohio."

"We have more than two whole weeks before they get back. All I have to do is make the breakfast and supper for you, wash the dishes, and keep the house clean, besides going to school," Susie explained.

"Besides helping me with the chores," Dannie reminded her. "That's the most important part."

"Ya well, we'll have our long winter evenings free to eat popcorn and apples and read books." Susie reached into the box, selected one and began to page through it. "This one is about a girl who came across the ocean with her mother to Penn's Woods in the 1700s. She kept a journal of all that happened to her. It sounds interesting."

"It's probably fiction," said a very unenthused Dannie. "In those days many of the immigrants couldn't even sign their own names. They put an 'X' beside the name someone else had written down for them. How could they have kept a journal? Even in Daniel Boone's time, people didn't have much schooling. Remember the time he marked the spot where he had killed a bear? With his knife he carved, 'D. Boone cilled a bar' into the tree. He had the words misspelled."

Susie was still reading. "It says there actually was such a girl. Her mother died on the voyage and was buried at sea. In Penn's Woods, the girl was captured by the Indians. She was rescued by a trapper whom she later married. She did keep a journal, but wrote only the barest facts. Someone then rewrote it, using their imagination to fill in details as they might have been. Parts of it were adapted from an old book written nearly a century ago."

"See . . . it's fiction," Dannie scoffed. "I'd rather read a true story any day. This *Cross Timbers Stories* book sure looks exciting."

"Aha!" Susie snickered. "Lewis B. Miller's books are fiction too, if you didn't know it."

"They are not," Dannie sounded indignant. "He writes of the pioneer times out west. Wolves, deer, buffalo, panthers, bears . . . and exciting stuff like that. Even Indians."

"But still fiction," Susie declared. "In the preface, it says the stories are tied to actual events and true-to-life. He blended historically accurate facts with fiction."

"That's good enough for me," Dannie said and returned to his book. "Even true stories of long ago can't be one hundred percent true, because the people's thoughts and conversations were made up by the author." He leaned back in his rocker and propped his feet on the range.

Susie nodded. "This book has some historical fiction, too. To me, it's interesting reading about those brave souls who came over to the New World and carved their lives out of the wilderness, especially in our state of Pennsylvania, or Penn's Woods, as they called it then." She stacked two pillows on the couch, curled up on it and began to read.

✍

DOROTHEA MARGUERITE'S JOURNAL BEGINS:

June 7: This finds me, Dorothea Marguerite, age 16, aboard the big ship, the *Charming Betsy*, headed for the new land of freedom and opportunity . . . America. Mother and I came aboard yesterday after passing all the wearisome inspections, and now we are on our way, setting sail on the busy Thames River.

Thanks to Madame Julius, the lady I used to do cleaning for, I am the grateful owner of a fine copybook, a full bottle of black walnut ink, and a supply of quills! She gave them to me as going away gifts the last time I scrubbed her floors. I am delighted to be able to keep a journal of our voyage and life in the new land. Mother also thinks it a very fine thing. She herself never mastered the art of spelling.

Yesterday's weather was beautiful, with a blue, blue sky filled with puffy white clouds. As we were walking along the wharf, watching the many ships and boats passing, Mother got one of her "tired" spells and wanted to catch her breath, so we sat down on a packing crate to rest. I begged to be allowed to explore a bit until it was time to board and Mother reluctantly gave her consent. It was an exciting place, alive with activity as the crewmen busily loaded provisions for the journey. I became so absorbed in watching the cheerful and lovely scene on the river (the sea vessels of many sizes and kinds, the dipping of oars, and the billow of sails in the picturesque blue and white sky) that I quite forgot to be careful. As I strolled along, I unexpectedly tripped over a coil of rope and felt myself falling in a most ungraceful and unladylike manner. Suddenly, a strong arm caught me and set me on my feet again. My cheeks blushed crimson when I saw the very fine young gentleman who had rescued me. He was wearing a suit made of the finest cloth and a jaunty three-cornered hat and bright buckles adorned his shoes.

"Careful there, young lady," he said crisply. But I couldn't help noticing the amused twinkle in his eyes and his twitching lips. His next words were, "May I have the honor of escorting you to your destination?" Without waiting for a reply, he linked his arm through mine—much to my embarrassment. Luckily, Mother came walking by just then and whisked me away, though I did manage a breathless "thank you" to the man. His reply was, "You're welcome, pretty one," making me blush all the more. I am sure that Mother was much displeased, thinking she'll not again trust me out of her sight. As soon as we were alone, she gave me yet another lengthy lecture on the dangers of associating too freely with strangers. I assured her roundly, that I had no intention of having my head turned by the charming flatterer, I would not be so easily swayed. But Mother is sure that I, at age 16, cannot realize the dangers this old world has to offer.

After that, there was the excitement of boarding the ship, being assigned berths, and putting away our meager store of belongings, that I quite forgot all about the young man. It was not until later in the evening, when Mother had given me permission to take a stroll on the deck to watch the sunset that he once again, like a ghost out of the twilight, appeared at my side. I was so flustered that I can't recall many of his charming, gracious words, only that he was very pleased to be sailing on the same vessel with me and would feel honored to accompany me in strolling on the deck. I was equally gracious to him, but I made my departure as soon as I politely could and hurried back to our room, hoping Mother wouldn't notice my flushed cheeks. I had no intentions of telling her I had once again met up with the friendly gentleman. I don't want her to be perturbed over a trifle or unduly concerned. She is not hardy and probably won't spend much time on deck, but I want to spend as much time as I can out there, for I don't think I could bear being cooped up inside much of the time. Later, as I lay on my berth being lulled to sleep by the gentle swaying and lapping of the water, I couldn't help but daydream a bit. After all, it is flattering to be noticed by a young man. But I brought myself up short when I thought of how much less attentive he would be when he found out how poor Mother and I are. I wondered what he will think when he finds out that we spent our last coins for new clothes for our journey and that we cannot as much as pay our own ship's fare. But, as I drifted off to sleep, I couldn't help but feel pleasantly excited about his accompanying us on our voyage. His name is Marquis Keith and he is five years older than I am.

I must lay this aside for now, for it is time for the noon meal. The bell is summoning us and I don't wish to be tardy.

June 8: I now take my quill pen in hand to resume where I left off yesterday. This morning, Mother had a headache so I was easily able to get her permission to let me take a stroll on the deck (after listening to her earnest admonishing about the company I keep. I assured her that she needn't worry. I was old enough to take care of myself. I stationed myself near the gangway, so enjoying the bracing fresh air and gentle sunshine that I was oblivious to my surroundings. Very soon, my devoted friend Marquis Keith, was there again, smiling his warm smile and presenting me with a brown paper-wrapped parcel. With trembling fingers, I undid the string and wrappings. I could not hide my delight when I found a string of fine-polished beads, but my eyes insisted on filling with tears. It was such a lovely gift, but I did not know if Mother would permit me to accept such a valuable gift from him. Bidding him wait, I carried it eagerly back to our room, hoping so much that Mother would say yes.

Mother was resting on her bunk with a cool washcloth on her forehead. Her eyes opened wide when she saw what I had in my hands. She declared it must be very valuable and at first in-sisted I must return the gift for it would not be proper to accept such a gift from a gentleman unless I was sure of returning his friendship, which she forbade. When I relayed the message to Marquis (as he asked me to call him), he seemed distressed and asked to speak to Mother himself. Finally, Mother came up on deck to meet Marquis. With his charming manner of speaking, he assured her that he is not trying to buy my friendship and requires nothing in return. The beads are not all that valuable; he bought them from a peddler for a song, he claimed, and I was to keep them, regardless. I didn't care all that much for the friend-ship (at least I think not) but I sure wanted the beads and put all the silent pleading I could into my eyes hoping Mother would relent. I never before had anything that was just for vanity.

Finally, she gave in, saying I could keep the gift if I would consent to only go up on deck when she did and stay by her side. It was a hard decision, but I wanted the beads at all costs and so I gave my word. After all, she is only trying to take good care of her "little" daughter and I am sure that after we are settled in our new home in America, she will relax her strict protectiveness and give me more freedom. She is a dear Mother—all I have since Father and my two little brothers died of the plague eight years ago. So, I will respect her "whims" and overlook her idiosyncrasies. Time to get back to knitting stockings.

✍

June 15: It hardly seems possible that a week has passed since my last journal entry. How time flies when one is enjoying the days. We have had smooth sailing so far, with brisk, but gentle winds billowing the sails and speeding us on our way. Whenever Mother and I go up on deck, without fail, the charming Marquis is soon at our side. He has made mention of my "mahogany-colored hair," as he called it. That's so much nicer than just plain "red." But, I suppose it is vanity to care about the color of one's hair.

I do believe Marquis is determined to win Mother's respect and approval by his immaculate manners, behavior, and pleasant helpfulness, so that she will relax her rules and allow us to stroll off by ourselves. Sometimes I find myself wishing he wouldn't be quite so determined, but then I feel guilty for my thoughts, remembering his generous gift. Also, at the back of my mind, is the thought that he doesn't know how poor we are and when he finds it out, he will seek out the friendship of another dame. I must mention it to him one of these days. Oh well, it was a rather pleasant diversion while it lasted, for surely it is just a passing fancy. Perhaps we'll never see each other again when we leave the ship. There is no use reading something into his attentiveness that isn't even there. Paper is patient, dear copybook, I'm sure you do not mind my ramblings which are intended for no other eyes.

A peaceful darkness is settling over the waters now and soon the myriad of stars will be twinkling overhead. Goodnight.

✍

June 21: I suppose if someone should pick up my copybook and read the lines I wrote, they would wonder how we are planning to cross this deep, wide ocean on a ship without any money at all. Well, it's this way: I have an uncle in America who will pay the fare. He wrote to Mother last fall, inviting us to come over. (The way he wrote, I think he may be interested in asking for Mother's hand in marriage. What will he say when he sees how frail she has become?) He sent us detailed instructions and wrote that he will meet us at the port in Philadelphia and pay our ship fare, then establish us in a home. This seemed like a dream come true to Mother, for her health is precarious and I think, is afraid that I will be left alone without a guardian. I was all for this exciting adventure too, willing to endure the hardships and dangers along the way.

Mother wrote back to Uncle Hendrick (who is my father's brother) at once, informing him of our plans. I've never seen Uncle Hendrick and Mother hasn't seen him for twelve years, so it will be quite a reunion. He is a trapper or trader and knows the New World as well as anyone.

By the way, I told our story of poverty to Marquis several days ago and now I haven't seen him since. I can't help but feel that I have gone down in his estimations since he knows. If such is the case, well, if material things make such a difference to him, perhaps he's not worth getting better acquainted with anyway. But still, my heart feels a bit sore and dissatisfied at the thought.

✍

June 25: Mother isn't feeling well so she gave me permission to go out for fresh air alone after all. The weather is bright and beautiful with sea gulls soaring in the blue sky. Large whales have been sighted in the distance as well as flying fish that jump high in the air. Close to the horizon, I see a fleet of ships ever so slowly coming closer. I do hope it's not pirate ships! Marquis is nowhere to be seen and I find myself missing him. The last time we saw a fleet of ships, he was with us, telling us where they probably hailed from and how big they would seem to us when they came closer.

Oh! There's Marquis now, walking across the deck, looking a bit pale and shaky. He's coming this way so I'll lay this aside for now.

LATER: Just goes to show how easy it is to jump to conclusions. Marquis has been ill these past few days, which was the reason why he stayed away, not because he despised our poverty, as I had mistakenly assumed. We sat on a piling and talked for quite awhile. He told me the story of his younger sister. She eloped with an older man at the age of 15. Her husband turned out to be an abusive tyrant and she was very unhappy. She died a year later, further breaking his widowed Mother's heart. (I think I'd better appreciate my mother's concern about being cautious in forming friendships with strangers. Mothers generally know best, I suppose, and have more insight than teenage girls.) But, Marquis does seem like a perfect gentleman. Besides, just because he gave me those beads does not mean he plans to steal away my heart!

On Sunday, a group of people held some kind of services here on deck, with a lengthy sermon and singing. Mother and I stayed away, I suppose it would have cost something to attend. We've never had good enough clothes to have much of a social life, until now.

I must go see how Mother is feeling. She looked so pale when I came out.

Susie reluctantly put her marker into the book and closed it. The clock on the mantle was striking nine. She closed her eyes, trying to imagine what it would have been like, traveling over the ocean on such a ship, depending on the wind and billowing sails, surrounded by the tossing waves, and miles and miles of water. Before she knew it, she was dozing off. The clock chiming 9:15 awakened her and she jumped up from her comfortable nest on the couch.

"Time for bed, Dannie," she said crisply. "I'll bank the fire for the night if you'll lock the doors. We don't want to over-sleep tomorrow morning."

Dannie tossed his book on the table, got out of his rocker and stretched himself. "Just when I was at the most exciting part," he grumbled. "Oh well, tomorrow's another day."

2

Heartaches and Tears

The next evening, the chores seemed to take extra long to Dannie and Susie. One of the hungry calves made an extra vigorous butt with its nose, spilling a nearly full bucket of milk replacer. He bawled hungrily while Susie disgustedly mixed another batch for him.

Then Dannie forgot to turn off the faucet at the steers' water trough and it overflowed. Finally, they were done and ready for more reading. Susie made a pot of cocoa and set a plate of butterscotch rolls on the table. She curled up on the couch with her book.

July 5: Yesterday, Mother and I sat on deck watching the porpoises jumping here and there, out of the water with a splash. The crewmen call them "storm fish," for their jumping is a forerunner of an approaching storm. And sure enough, this morning the wind is picking up and the skies are threatening rain. I hope it won't be too bad, for Mother's sake, for she gets seasick so easily and hasn't an ounce of flesh to spare. She's becoming weary of seeing water all around us, as far as anyone can see . . . water and more water, with the ship rocking on the swells. I don't blame her for it, because everything is so much harder to take when one doesn't feel well. Last week we stopped at the Isle of Wight, in the English Channel to refuel the ship. We gazed longingly at the picturesque rock and thatch houses in Cowes. Along the winding streets the blooming roses spilled over low stone walls. The green grass in the yards and the blooms in the window boxes looked so inviting. The steep, gabled roofs and the chimneys brought back memories of home and I had to brush away a few tears.

But, of course, there was no turning back now.

We never speak of our fears and misgivings, but they are always there, threatening to overwhelm us. We always speak of better days ahead in America, where we'll have no more worries about where our next meal comes from and we'll have relief from our poverty. Uncle Hendrick will provide for us there. I think, that unless he has some ulterior motives, he must be a very kind man.

I dare not complain to Mother, for she has enough to bear, but I'm getting so tired of ship's fare and so tired of doing nothing but knitting. No wonder I welcome Marquis' company as a diversion. Time to lay this aside, for the wind is getting stronger and the waves higher. Rain lashes against our feeble craft and the hatches must be kept closed. Soon it will be utterly dark in here. Poor Mother!

July 6: Poor Mother indeed! She lies with her head near a basin. The rain is still coming down relentlessly and the powerful wind is creating stiff waves that rock our feeble craft mercilessly. I am not feeling well myself, for the endless heaving and pitching never ceases. It makes my head spin round and round. I find myself longing to be back in my little old chimney corner in our humble home, where I could creep to my mat and be at peaceful rest.

July 13: The weather is calm again, but Mother is no better. If only there were a proper physician aboard this vessel, maybe he could do something for her. There is one along that goes by that name, but he has been known to make people feel worse rather than better. It's hard to see one's dear Mother suffer so. I alternate between sitting with my head buried in my apron, weeping piteously, and pacing the deck like a caged animal. When she is awake, I bathe her fevered brow and sing to her if I am able to manage it, without my voice breaking and quavering. I must be strong for her sake, but to see her flushed cheeks and glazed, sunken eyes seems to drain every ounce of strength from me. Sometimes her mind wanders and her hands ceaselessly pluck at the covers as if she thinks she is plucking the feathers from a chicken. Oh Mother! Mother! If only I could help her, but it's no use. If there is a God above, may He hear my cry and help us.

July 14: Mother was more lucid today and had the strength to talk. "Dear daughter," she said, "I fear, nay, rather, I know I am not long for this world. You must prepare yourself and be strong."

But I couldn't bear to have her talk so. "Hush Mother," I cried. "You are not going to die." I was terrified by the thought. "You must get well." I threw myself upon her and we clasped each other in a convulsive embrace while our sobs echoed from the walls in a violent burst of grief. I fear I would not have been able to stop had not the thought of how it must be making Mother worse brought me to my senses. I knelt beside her and laid my face close to hers on the pillow, softly stroking her cheek until she fell asleep. Then I crept away, running blindly to the end of the ship where I found a hiding place in a cubby hole under the stairs where no one could see me. My frame shook with silent sobs as the tears flowed. "Oh Mother, Mother," I inwardly wailed. "How could you do this to me? I'll be all alone in a strange land." The more I tried to stifle my sobs, the more the pent up emotions and tempest of grief shook me afresh, until I thought I would die and even wished I would. I wondered wildly how I'd ever be able to stop, until I heard someone calling my name. "Dorothea Marguerite, whatever is the matter? Why are you hiding under the stairs?" It was Marquis, bending over to peek into my hiding place, his eyes looking very kind and concerned. Before I could stop myself, I was, between sobs, pouring out my sad, sad story to him of my mother's illness and the dread of having to arrive all alone on the shores of America without my dear mother.

Marquis gave me a clean white handkerchief and waited until all my sobs had subsided, then said, "Your mother may get well after all and if she doesn't, you may come with me to my mother's home in Philadelphia. She is a good, kind, motherly person and will take care of you, I know. You would love her I'm sure . . . everybody does."

That made me remember my uncle and I thanked him for his kind offer, saying I hoped it wouldn't be necessary, then hurried back to Mother's side. She lay as if in a coma, barely breathing. Seeing there was nothing I could do for her, I poured out my feelings in my copybook. I plan to stay up with her all night, doing what I can for her care and comfort.

Later: It seems I have lost all track of time. I move around as one in a daze. Is it all true, or only a bad dream? Did I really see them take Mother's body and put it into a canvas shroud, ready to heave it over the side of the ship into the relentless waves of water? Was it me who flung myself at them to prevent them? Whose were those strong hands that caught me and drew me back? Was it Marquis or was it just all a faraway dream? I remember someone reciting a prayer and then she was gone, far beneath the foaming brine, gone forever and ever. I remember hearing wails (my own) and then someone was spooning laudanum into my mouth. Next I knew, I thought I was the one in the sea. Waves of drowsiness swept over me and I was in a sea of calm. I slept I don't know how long, but it was a merciful sleep, erasing everything else. Perhaps I shall soon go to join Mother.

August: We have been on the ocean forever and ever. There was no beginning and there is no end. We have been becalmed and making no progress day after day. I feel so very ill, so tired and weak. The drinking water on board has become stale and covered with thick black scum. Before drinking, someone skims the worms off the top of the water and no one drinks more than they have to. Many are sick and many have already died. The broiling summer sun scorches us all and the children cry piteously for a drink of fresh water. The sound of moaning and weeping echoes throughout the ship. Hunger, thirst, and fatigue make us all short-tempered and irritable. Oh, how we long to be back home. Would that God send a terrific storm and capsize the ship, burying us all at sea? This afternoon I heard someone begging for a drop, just one drop of fresh water, followed by moans and weeping. I feebly groped my way to the sound. I was horrified to find that it was Marquis, tossing and turning in his bunk and quite delirious. Oh, why did he have to get so sick too? I felt as if he was my last friend on the earth (or the sea). Sometimes his reason would return for a short time and he would beg for fresh water. His eyes were sunken too, just like Mother's had been. I was standing there staring in horrified silence, when suddenly his eyes cleared and he said, "Oh Dorothea Marguerite, here you are at last. I was hoping to see you before I die. Open my satchel, there's a parcel there for Mother and I want you to take it to her when you arrive in Philadelphia. Can I trust you to take care of it for me?" His eyes searched mine wildly and then he was off in another fit of delirium, raving senselessly. I felt too weak to take another step, but forced myself to the corner where his satchel lay. I opened it and there on the top lay the parcel. I knew it was the right one, for the words, "Mother—Hannah Keith" were written on it. I took it to my bunk, wondering if I will live to reach the City of Brotherly Love.

Two Days Later: I watched the crewmen heave the body of Marquis Keith overboard tonight. I thought of his mother waiting eagerly for her son to come home, not knowing she will never see him again on the face of the earth. My own heart felt dead— numb. I couldn't feel anything. I was too drained, too void of emotion.

Many are dying of dysentery, others are seasick day after day. The ship's crewmen do nothing to clean up the mess, for there is no extra water for washing. Rats are swarming everywhere and the stench and fumes are enough to make anyone sick. Lice, boils, scurvy, malnutrition, and mouth rot plague us all. I feel miserably sick. Last night I dreamt I was walking in verdant, green pastures beside still blue waters in a beautiful place where all is peace and joy and there is no pain.

✍

September: I know not what day of the month it is, but I believe we are nearing land. I hear excited voices and a great swelling through the ship. The captain told us last week that the

sight of land will make the half dead alive again, but sometimes I wonder if I will ever feel alive again. Without Mother I have no joy in arriving in the new land. I would rather be back in our old home, in the little chimney corner where I could rest. But now the cry of Land! Land! is ringing through the ship and many are weeping, shouting, or singing. Perhaps I will drag myself up on deck after all.

Susie laid the book aside, tears filling her eyes. *How much worse can it get*, she wondered. *Oh, how I pity those weary, heartsick ones. What will Dorothea Marguerite do now, arriving in a strange new land all alone without a mother, father, brother, or sister?*

3

Arriving at Philadelphia

The next evening, just as Susie and Dannie had settled down to read, they heard a knock on the door. "Looks like it's our old friend Wynn," Dannie said happily. "Susie, you better make some more popcorn and fetch more cider." He went to the door and called out, "Come on in and join the party!"

The rosy-cheeked old man went to the stove to warm his hands. "Smells good in here with freshly popped corn and birch logs on the fire. Brings back memories of my childhood."

"Tell us stories about your childhood," Susie wheedled, handing him a glassful of cider. Wynn needed no second invitation. He launched into one fascinating story after another and before they knew it, an hour had passed and it was time for Wynn to go.

"Thanks for the most interesting evening," Dannie said. "That sure beats reading storybooks."

Especially sad ones like I'm reading, Susie thought. *I pity those people so.* She got her book down from the shelf and turned to the page where she'd left her marker.

✍

October 1: It feels good to have solid land under one's feet, to see the beautiful trees, and hear birds twittering. But where is Uncle Hendrick? The confusing babble of German, English, Irish, and Dutch languages all around me makes my head ache. If only I'd feel well and strong for I still feel so ill. My heart goes out to those who came over as indentured servants or redemptioners, for only now do they realize the pain of being separated from the rest of their families, even spouses sometimes. Torn apart and sold, maybe never to find each other again after their term of service is over. I greatly fear my lot will be the same if Uncle doesn't show up soon. Where could he be? What if he was killed or something? Someone has to pay the fare, for if no one does, I'll be put up on the auction block for sure. Just a short time ago, a man with a ragged scar on his cheek and a leer on his face came by, ogling over me. He stared at me from head to foot, then said loudly, "If no one has spoken payment for this redhead here, I'll pay her fare. She'll make good bride material after she gets some flesh on her bones."

Though trembling with indignation, I mustered all the strength I could and said, with more confidence than I felt, "My uncle will be along any moment to pay my fare!" But I feel so very alone. Why, oh why, doesn't he come? One thought consoles me, those who don't pass the health inspection will be taken to the Sick House. There I would be safe, for awhile, at least. Oh God, if You are up there, help me now.

October 2: I have been weeping for joy this past hour, which I suppose is also partly a reaction from the terrible strain I've been through since we reached land. What fears rolled through my mind as I waited and wondered what would happen to me. When Uncle Hendrick did not show up at all, I thought I would faint with anxiety. What's more, though I felt as ill as ever, the physician gave me a stamp of health, saying that I was just ill from seasickness and malnutrition and that plenty of good food and fresh air would cure me. So I had not even the hope of being sent to the Sick House. The bold scar-faced man came back again and grinning broadly, began to make negotiations with the captain for paying my fare. I was in utmost despair, not knowing what to do and began to heave loud sobs. Just then a voice as sweet as an angel's spoke in my ear and I felt a kind hand on my shoulder. A kind, middle-aged lady was bending over me asking what the trouble was. Like a person drowning, I clung to her for a lifeline, pouring out my terrible fears and crying unashamedly. I was past caring and unable to control my emotions.

The angel lady gave Scar Face a black look and informed him firmly that **she** was paying my fare and taking me with her and that he must be gone with his wicked intentions and evil scheming or she would report him to the authorities. Her words were effective, for he turned on his heel and slunk away through the crowds.

"Come child." The kind lady pulled me to my feet and "took me under her wings." She helped me to sign my name on the mayor's document, then took me to the State House to take the Oath of Allegiance & Abjuration. She did not speak much after that, for tears kept filling her eyes and flowing down over her cheeks. She seemed to be in a great sadness of her own that I knew nothing about. I felt overwhelmed with gratefulness for her kindness in inviting me to her home and though I still felt faint and ill, was able to keep up with her as we walked the cobblestone street to her home. My spirits had lifted so much that I was able to take in the fascinating sights and sounds around me: the brick houses with cedar-shingled roofs and plate glass windows, the hitching posts out front, and the garden pavilions. We passed a printer's shop, a glass foundry, and a blacksmith shop. Trees swayed in the breeze and the smell of the river wafted over the streets from the dockside area. We passed and met many people in this busy, bustling place . . . men and women dressed in English fashions; ladies wearing beautifully decorated bonnets and velvet, lace-trimmed gloves; and men with powdered wigs and silver-buckled shoes. We turned in at a large, elegant brick home set far back from the street, surrounded by beautiful trees in their fall colors. A stone statue of a boy holding aloft a whale oil lantern presided over the pavilion. The steps up to the veranda were of flat inlaid stones. The lady lifted the iron latch of the massive oak door and ushered me inside. A rush of gentle warmth enveloped me. There was a crackling fire of hickory logs on the hearth. What a sweet luxury to lie down on a soft feather bed in that cheerful warmth! My tears insisted on flowing, and thankfully the angel lady didn't seem to notice for her own tears were thick on her cheeks. After awhile, she came over to me with a peeled and sliced apple on a plate. Sweet wonder of wonders! My appetite had returned and I savored every tangy, delicious bite. It tasted like ambrosia after the ship's unpalatable fare and more tears flowed. Will I ever stop crying about every little joy and goodness that comes my way?

✍

October 3: Soon after I finished my last journal entry, the kind lady came over to me, graciously extending her hand.

"Please forgive me, I haven't even told you my name, nor told you why I am so consumed with sadness. I'm Hannah Keith. I was expecting my son home on the *Charming Betsy.*" Her voice broke. "He was one of those buried at sea."

Her tears fell thick and fast and suddenly, a light dawned on my face. Hannah Keith! "Oh! You must be Marquis Keith's mother!" I gasped. "I hadn't suspected . . ." Then we were both talking at once, I explaining about Marquis befriending me on the ship and she asking questions and wondering and hanging onto every word. She wanted me to tell her all I knew about her son, so hungry she was for word about him. It wasn't until later that I remembered the parcel in my satchel, which Marquis had given for her. When I handed it to her, more tears flowed down over her cheeks and she went into the other room to be alone with it. I know just how she felt, for I too, cherish every thought and remembrance of my dear departed one.

✍

October 10: Every day I find myself getting stronger, all from eating Hannah Keith's good food. There are roasts of beef, rounds of cheese, succulent baked beans, creamy baked dried corn, crusty loaves of bread, celery from her garden, and all the shiny red apples I care to eat. What bliss! Resting on her fine featherbeds has also refreshed me. Now I find myself wanting to get out and walk, to see more of this bustling city and to find some worthwhile work to do. I can't believe the energy I have! Hannah and I go out walking every afternoon to see the sights and activities all around us. I feel like I can never get enough of the crisp, fresh, leaf-scented air. Hannah says the air is full of foul city smells, but to me it is fresh. Will I ever be able to forget the stench of the ship?

We walked down to the State House again, for I was too ill to notice much last time. It's the most splendid building I've ever seen! It must be all of 100 feet long, with sparkling plate glass windows in the front. On the outside of the south front, there's a huge square stair tower. It is very high with four chimneys at both ends and a banister along the roof. It's all so very rich and grand! If only Mother could be here with me, enjoying all these awesome sights. I've seen brick kilns, tannery yards, iron and glass foundries, mercantile shops, and sawyers rigs. Down on the broad Delaware River there are ships bringing spices, sugar, tea, rice, molasses, fine cloth, flour, and flax seed from many places in the Old World. Fluttering from the masts of the ships there are flags from the East and West Indies, Portugal, Spain, Ireland, Scotland, England, Holland, and many other places. At night the lights from many whale oil lamps light up the streets. I love to go up Mrs. Keith's broad stairway to a second floor window to see all the twinkling lights. Surely there has never been a city with so many!

I'm saving the best of all until last to write. Hannah Keith told me tonight she wants to adopt me as her own daughter! It seems too good to be true! That is, until I think of at what awful cost this portion is to be mine. I would rather have my own dear mother back, even though we'd have to live in a poor log cabin, than have all the fine clothes, riches, comforts, luxuries, and grand mansions this world has to offer. But she will never come back and I must make the best of what comes my way. Time to say "Goodnight," dear journal, but I fear I shall be too excited to sleep.

✍

October 17: How fast one's plans can change and one's dream castles come crashing down to the ground. Yesterday, late afternoon just before supper, there came a brisk knock on the door. Hannah was busy with supper preparations and thinking it might be a peddler, asked me to go see who was there. On the stone step stood a man wearing a broad-rimmed hat, plain homespun clothes, wide suspenders, and shoes made of cowhide. He doffed his hat, asking, "Is this Hannah Keith's abode? May I speak to her, please?"

Hearing his voice, Hannah came to the door and I went to see to supper. Hannah invited the man to take a seat by the hearth, then called to me to join them. "A message for you," she half whispered. A stab of apprehension pierced my heart, wondering what was to come. Was it another fellow like the bold scar-faced man?

The man extended his hand to me and in kindly tones said, "I am Christian Herr from Neu-Strasburge way, here with a message from one Hendrick Karmenson, who claims to be your uncle. He sends word that he chopped himself in the foot with his ax a fortnight ago and is unable to travel. He asks that you come with my wife and I to our home to await his arrival there, which in all likelihood, will be in several weeks."

Seeing my gasp of dismay, Hannah encircled me with her arm. "I will invite them to stay for supper," she said in a low voice. "We will further discuss this afterward."

Christian and his wife, Anna, (who had been sitting on the seat of the Herr's big covered wagon, awaiting her husband's return) accepted Hannah's invitation to stay. After putting their horses into the barn, they came to the house together. I quickly helped Hannah slice more bread and cheese and we added more milk to the pumpkin soup and put more fat cakes on the plate. When pleasant-faced Anna Herr came into the kitchen, she smiled brightly and I felt instinctively that one could not help but like her.

"This is so kind of you to invite us in to your table," she said gratefully, shaking hands with both of us. "A warm supper will taste good after traveling so far. I'm so glad we found your house so easily. When we inquired down at the docks, we learned of your mother's passing, Dorothea Marguerite. You have our deepest sympathy." Her eyes mirrored her compassion and I knew she was not just trying to be polite. She went on, "At first, no one seemed to know what had become of you. But then a man with a deep scar on his face told us you were here and gave directions. *Gott sie dank!*"

Scar Face again. I nearly gasped. He knew where I was. What if he tried to make more trouble for me? For a moment I wished he had not told them where I was, for I didn't like the idea of leaving Hannah for an unknown destiny. I felt sure that I could trust the Herrs, but leaving this safe harbor at the Keith home was heart wrenching. What if Uncle Hendrick was a crude, uncouth man? What is the life of a trapper and trader like anyway? What if he doesn't have a proper home? Thoughts like these tumbled over each other in my head as we did the dishes, then found seats in the parlor to visit.

Hannah invited the Herrs to stay and spend the night there too, which they gratefully accepted, apparently glad that they would not have to go seeking lodgings at an inn. The Herrs planned to start for their home tomorrow and they have room for me in their wagon. After discussing the matter for over an hour, we came to the conclusion that it is best that I go with the Herrs. Hannah assured me that if life with Uncle Hendrick is less than desirable, her home is always open to me and that she will welcome me back with open arms. What a comforting thought! She insisted on giving me a satchel containing a complete set of clothes for me. Her eyes filled with tears as she packed the clothes. These had belonged to her daughter, the girl who had eloped with an older man and died a year later, which Marquis had told me about. She also put in a thick, wool winter shawl and a full bottle of black walnut ink. How kind and generous she is!

We (the Herrs and I) will start off early tomorrow morning for their home and I must be ready at the crack of dawn. They come to Philadelphia every fall, to sell barrels of cider and as soon as their business transactions are done, they want to get back to their five children: John, Christian, Abraham, Elizabeth, and Anna and to their Grosdaudy, Hans Herr. I can feel it in my bones that there are exciting adventures ahead of me, but whether they are for good or for ill, I do not know. Will we see Indians or wild animals such as bears, deer, or panthers? Hannah Keith is such a dear soul and staying in her home has been such a pleasant blessing. The Herrs are very nice too, but I just wish I'd know what my uncle is like.

Time to get to bed, whether to sleep or to toss restlessly remains to be seen. Goodnight.

✍

When the clock bonged nine times, Susie closed her book and laid it back on the shelf. *Things are looking up for Dorothea Marguerite*, she thought happily. *First a kind friend like Hannah Keith and now the Herrs. I'm so glad that bold scar-faced man didn't get her. She's looking forward to adventures in Penn's Woods and I do wonder what all she'll have to face.*

4

At the Herr's House

The next day was Sunday. Dannie hitched Rusty to the *dach-vegli*, and he and Susie drove the two miles to church. The afternoon was spent with friends who persuaded them to stay for supper. So it was late when they finally got started with the chores and then afterward, there was a letter for Susie to write to her sister, Nancy. She had just happened to think of something.

Well, well! Susie thought to herself. *Now I know where I've heard of the Herrs before. Christian built a stone house in*

1719, which has been restored and is now called the Hans Herr House. That's the place Nancy and Andrew visited last fall, back home in Pennsylvania. I must write to Nancy and tell her about this story. I'll do it right away and ask her to write back to tell me all she knows about the place.

Susie got out her pen and stationary and before the clock struck nine, had her letter in the envelope, sealed, and stamped. She looked forward to hearing from Nancy and Andrew soon. And so, it wasn't until Monday evening that Susie opened her book again.

✍

October 18: Twilight is descending and I will have to write fast if I wish to record the day's happenings before darkness overtakes me. We (the Herrs and I) started off early this morning in the big covered wagon drawn by two sturdy horses. We traveled all day as planned and have now found a place to camp for the night, in a grassy meadow by a creek. We're under the spreading branches of a giant sycamore tree with the creek waters murmuring by. On the other side of the creek is a wooded ridge, with the rosy red glow of the sunset shining through the still colorful trees. We saw many such beautiful trees today, decked in crimsons, gold, browns, and greens.

We had hardly gone more than a mile or so when we forded the big Schuylkill River. I was thankful it was autumn instead of spring, for Anna Herr told me that with the springtime rains and snowmelt, the waters are high and raging. Oftentimes the horses lose their footing and have to swim against a strong current. Just this past spring, a man lost his life when an unseen whirlpool swept his horse off course and pulled him into the treacherous depth.

We rode through mostly wooded areas, occasionally passing sturdy cabins and cleared land; some with rustling corn shocks and piles of pumpkins. At one cabin, a girl on a horse waved to me and I wished I could stop and make her acquaintance. Then it was more woodland and hills. We saw such spectacular scenery that it filled my heart with awe at the grandeur of it.

Christian Herr has now started a cheerily blazing fire over which Anna is cooking our supper. I offered to help, but she kindly told me to rest instead, knowing that I am still somewhat rundown from our ocean voyage. The rich aroma of coffee bubbling in the coffeepot and mush frying in the pan whets my appetite. I know I shall soon be stout and hardy again if I continue to have such wholesome and ample fare. Breathing the fresh, crisp fall air might have something to do with getting extra hungry, too.

Christian has unhitched the horses from the wagon and tethered them, allowing them to crop the still lush green grass. He talked to them friendly-like, as though they were able to understand and they nickered companionably in reply. Never before have I been so close to such fine horses! Before I settled on this log to write, I (with Christian's permission) went over to them and stroked their shining necks. They must have liked it, for they nudged me with their velvet muzzles and nickered contentedly.

It feels good to rest, for traveling over rutted roads is tiresome. Anna Herr told me that they usually don't have the white, billowing top over the wagon, but have put it on for this trip because of the possibility of rainy weather. It's good to know we won't have to get soaked if it rains tonight or tomorrow. After selling all their cider, they filled the wagon with supplies they bought at the mercantile for other settlers whose farms they pass on the way home

A gentle twilight is settling down over our cozy campsite. A hoot owl's quavering notes echo from a tree on the ridge, and from afar I heard a strange barking which the Herrs said is a fox. What a good feeling it is to be traveling with trustworthy people like the Herrs. While the birds twitter their goodnights, darkness descends as they find their resting places. Anna has just announced that the vittles are ready and I don't want to make

them wait. Always before eating, they bow their heads for a silent, reverent prayer of thanks. It makes God seem so real and very close.

October 20: I will now take time to write about our arrival at Christian and Anna Herr's homestead. Or perhaps I should write "at Hans Herr's house" for Christian's father Hans (or Grosdaudy as they call him), who is a widower and the patriarch of the family, lives here with his son and family. Though he is aged and somewhat feeble, he still seems to be the head of the house. He has long, gray hair curled under at the ends and parted in the middle, a full beard, and heavy brows. When I entered the *küche* (as Anna calls her kitchen) where he sat by the fire, he had a kindly smile and welcome for me and I felt as if I had found another friend. The children greeted me with shy, welcoming smiles as well. As we drove into the *vorhof* (the space between the house and the barn) they came running from the house to greet us. First came the three boys: John, Christian, and Abraham, who are 9, 7, and 5. Following were the three-year-old Elizabeth and baby Anna, who just recently learned to toddle about on her sturdy little legs. I wanted to scoop her up in my arms, but she clung to her mother and even little Elizabeth shyly hid in her mother's skirts. How happy they all seemed to have their parents come home, though they had surely been well taken care of by an aunt and uncle in their parents' absence. But no one can take the place of Mother. My own heart throbbed painfully at the thought of not being able to ever again greet my dear mother. At the most unexpected times, the memories and the sorrow hit me full force again and the grief nearly overwhelms me.

The boys plied their parents with questions, wanting to know every detail of the trip. They sat down—Anna holding the two little girls and the boys gathered 'round their dad—telling them all they wanted to know. They are such a dear, close-knit family. I feel as if I couldn't remain sad for very long in such warm, comfortable surroundings. It truly is a haven of peace, as every home ought to be.

Let me write a bit about the dwelling itself. I was quite impressed as we rode in the lane, seeing the house surrounded by the many apple trees. It's on a rise overlooking the creek and the springs, built tall and solid of stones rather than logs. The roof has Germanic-style side-lapped shingles that keep out the rain. No need to fear that a bear or wolf will be able to come out of the forest of oak trees surrounding the Herr homestead and somehow get into the house. I believe I shall feel quite safe here.

When we entered the *stube* (as they call the main room), I was surprised at how plain and bare it was, not at all fancy or extravagant. There's a built-in corner bench, or *eck bank* as the Herrs say. Also a masonry stove of brick and plaster, a small corner cupboard, a case clock, and a table with benches. In the *küche* is a huge central fireplace with a raised hearth, and a massive wood fire crane above it. There was a savory smelling stew bubbling in a pot suspended from the crane, while filling the kitchen with its wonderful aroma.

Anna showed me a small room just off the *k, che*, which she called the *kammerli*. It is to be my bedroom while I stay with the Herrs. She took me up the winding stairs and showed me where the boys sleep. From there, massive steps, each strewn out of a single log, lead up to the second attic, where grain is sometimes stored and the *schnitzelbank*, or shaving bench is kept. All the oak shingles for the roof were made on the *schnitzelbank*. After supper, I wandered out to the barn where the children's uncle was shoeing a horse. I watched for awhile as he worked the bellows and heated a horseshoe until it was red hot, then shaped it on the anvil, the sparks flying as he hammered. He then hitched the horse to his wagon and he and his wife left for home. I came inside then to record the day's events in my copybook. As I entered the door, I saw what I had missed seeing the first time. Christian had carved his initials and the date (1719) into the stone lintel over the front door. I think this house is built so solidly that it can withstand the strongest winds. I believe it could even stand for 100 years or more if the world stands that long. I'm sure it would be a real fortress against marauding Indians. But Anna Herr tells me that a man named William Penn has made a peace treaty with the Indians and that they are very friendly. So, all my fears about Indians were for nothing. The light is fading from the window and I must lay this aside for now.

October 27: Everyday I am feeling more and more at home here with the Herrs. Christian has sent word with Peter Bazaillion, who is an acquaintance of Uncle Hendrick's and has the same occupation, that I am here awaiting his arrival and also of the passing of my mother. I am, on one hand, anxious to see my uncle and on the other hand, dreading it. What kind of life will I have with him? If he invited us over to the New World with the idea of asking for my mother's hand in marriage, will he want to be bothered with providing for just me now? What if he only had selfish motives in the matter? Oh well, it's no use worrying about it yet.

The Herrs are such good, kind people. They spend their time very religiously and industriously, by saying prayers morning and evening and by having services here in the *stube* every Sunday, which Anna Herr said is "for the benefit of the Most High" or maybe she meant for the benefit of the people worshipping the Most High. The settlers come from far and near to hear the preaching and to join in the singing of psalms. Their worship appears to be serious and devout; peaceful Anabaptist folks who live to be a blessing and good example to others.

On Sunday, Grosdaudy Hans preached the first sermon, which was not very long, then Christian preached the main sermon. I listened intently and found myself wondering why my mother had never taught me more of these things. Maybe it was because we were too poor to have decent clothes in which to go to church. My grandmother Marguerite, for whom I was named, had a strong faith in God and tried to teach me about Him. I wish now I'd have taken her teachings more to heart and asked more questions before she died five years ago. My eyes overflowed with tears and a great longing for such a glorious faith and hope filled my heart. After the services were over, we had a meal no different from our usual everyday fare: course bread, venison, turnips cooked in broth, beans sweetened with molasses and baked on the hearth, applesauce, and cornbread. I had so longingly hoped for a family to arrive with a girl my own age, but there was none. Many have small children, but there were a few boys both older and younger than myself, one girl age 12, and one age 10. There was a young bride a few years older than myself, but when I spoke to her I felt we hadn't much in common and couldn't think of much to say.

✍

October 28: Colder weather is coming. A few flakes of flying snow fell as I helped Anna with the washing this morning. Afterward, as I warmed my hands at the raised hearth, Grosdaudy Hans, from his chair by the fire, spoke to me and asked me if I had understood any of the sermon on Sunday. I sat on the chair he offered me and baby Anna came running to me to be held. He was in a talkative mood. I believe he feels it is his duty to find out the condition of my soul and to lead me to the truth. And I am open to it, for I find myself drawn to their faith and their peaceable ways. If Christ died for me, as Grosdaudy Hans claims, and wants to lead me to Heaven through His Holy Spirit, then I want to know more about it. He told me the story of the persecution the martyrs went through and how they died for their faith. How well grounded they must have been in their faith to be willing to lay down their lives for it! How I wish I'd have such a strong faith. I am looking forward to next Sunday's sermons and also to having more talks with Grosdaudy Hans in the evenings when the work is done.

Early this morning before the sun was up, I took the kitchen bucket and went through the frosty morning to the springhouse for water so Anna could cook porridge. As I was walking down the slope, I saw a rustling of the bright sumac leaves at the edge of the woods and out stepped two young deer. They looked so peaceful and unafraid that I wanted to walk up to them and pat their graceful necks. But just then Christian came up the lane with the cow and away bounded the deer, their up-raised white tails disappearing in the brush. Christian called to me and asked if I wanted to learn how to milk the cow. Indeed I did! He fed the cow, then sat on a milk stool and showed me how to direct the stream of frothy milk into the bucket. It looked so easy until I tried it! I was pulling and squeezing wrong. Anna walked into the barn just then and patiently gave me more in-structions and demonstrations. Soon I had the knack of it, al-though my arms and hands were very tired. I am getting stron-ger everyday, though, and Anna says my cheeks are getting rosier and my eyes sparklier. No wonder, for there is plenty of whole-some food on the table and pure water and fresh air aplenty. Thinking of our ship's fare makes me gag even yet. Time to lay this aside, for Anna is ready to make butter and cheese and I want to learn how to do it, too.

Susie glanced at the clock. Bedtime so soon. She yawned and placed the book on the shelf. *So Dorothea Marguerite is learning to milk a cow,* she mused. *I wonder what it would seem like to be able to turn back the clock nearly 300 years and step into life as it was then. People back then didn't have to worry about highway accidents or nuclear bombs. But they had to face many trials and dangers that we don't have, I'm sure. I hope Nancy writes back soon and tells me more about the Hans Herr House. I think it has been restored to its original appearance and is now open to the public. I hope I get to see it someday.*

✍

5

In the Heart of Penn's Woods

Susie poured a half cup of popcorn kernels into the wire corn popper, then removed a lid from the cookstove and placed it over the fire. As soon as she heard the first pop, she began to vigorously shake the basket. One by one the kernels began to pop and leap, then faster and faster until the basket was filled. She shuffled the fluffy white kernels into a bowl and then poured the caramel syrup she had cooked over top of it.

"Yum!" Danny sniffed appreciatively as he came in the door, bringing a draft of cold air with him. "I hope you made plenty."

"I made two batches," Susie told him. "But don't eat it all. I want to take some along to school; enough for the girls in my class."

Both Susie and Dannie munched on the popcorn as they resumed reading the books they had chosen. The fire crackled in the range and the tea kettle whistled as the winds howled outside and rattled the windows. But they soon became so absorbed in their stories that they were oblivious to their surroundings.

✍

October 29: I went for a walk in the woods this morning with the three little boys; John, Christian, and Abraham. We saw several wild turkeys strutting about warily. They flew away noisily when seven-year-old Christli (as they call him) threw a pebble in their direction. Also a ring-necked pheasant and a few hens went strolling through the thickets. Frisky little bushy-tailed gray squirrels darted here and there among the tree branches, chattering mightily. They raced up and down the trees, some with nuts in their mouths. Nine-year-old Abraham said they're gathering the nuts to store for their food supply for the winter. The leaves are now mostly off the trees, although here and there remain colorful splashes, making nice scenery. Anna says that soon the icy winds of winter will blow and the snow will fly and pile up in big drifts. Tonight while we were gathered around the table we heard a wolf howling from a distant ridge. Christian says the wolves are partial to sheep, and as for the bears—they like pork just as well as we people do—and can carry off a good-sized pig. I'm glad for this good, solid stone house where we can be safely sheltered from hungry wild beasts.

I have to wonder when Uncle Hendrick will come for me. If I have to go, I hope it will be before the winter snows arrive.

✍

October 30: I had another talk with Grosdaudy Hans tonight as we sat by the fire shelling a bushel of roasted corn to be made into mush. He says the Pequea Valley and beyond is a

land flowing with milk and honey, but the most precious thing we have here is religious freedom. According to him, the Switzers (as others in the New World call them) have suffered much for their faith, first in Switzerland where they originated from, and where many were burned at the stake, drowned, and killed with the sword. However, the government was soon to learn that executing the re-baptizers did not prevent the rapid increase of their numbers. They had a living hope and did not fear a martyr's death. Their inner peace and joy while going to their deaths was noticed by the bystanders who had come to watch the executions. They witnessed the calm inner strength that came from a power beyond themselves, and wanted for themselves what the martyrs had.

I feel the same way when I see the way the Herrs live—sincere and above reproach. They believe in adult baptism upon their confession of faith, rather than infant baptism, and that the Holy Spirit helps them to resist worldly temptations and fleshly lusts, and helps them to live a life of righteousness, peacefulness, and quiet joyfulness. Grosdaudy Hans is old and feeble now, but his voice rings with the conviction of a strong inner faith. I wish I dared ask him how I can be cleansed of my sins and have this glorious faith too. But perhaps I am too unworthy and insignificant. In thinking back over my life, I see much of self-will, petulance, and mischievousness. Mother used to accuse me of "making provocative eyes" sometimes, which I declare was not true. I simply could not help it if my eyes danced when I chatted with someone and it made no difference if it was a girl or a boy. But I know I've too often been shallow and silly—not at all serious-minded. Now I'd like to be a child of God, so that if a bear or wolf tears me to pieces, or I'm shot through by an Indian arrow, or drowned in a raging river, I'd go straight to the Saviour in Heaven. Anna Herr talks much of trusting in the Lord and dwelling within His will, wherein lies divine care and protection.

It's time now to lay this aside and go to my narrow bed in the *kammerli*. Christian just came in from doing the chores, bringing a gust of cold air with him saying, "It's an air that smells of coming snow. I believe our warm Indian summer weather has ended for this harvest season." Goodnight.

✍

November 1: During the night I heard the wind howling around the corners of the house and the chimney, flinging the snowflakes against the window. Anna had given me an extra cover, but I was still shivering, so I knew the temperature had dropped way down. I heard voices in the *stube*, so I hurriedly dressed, wondering if my uncle had come. Instead, when I unsuspectingly walked through the door into the room, I was greeted by the sight of half a dozen Indian braves. I gasped and might have screamed, but Anna quickly encircled me with her arm, explaining that the Indians are on perfect terms of friendship with them. They often come to the house with fish and venison in exchange for bread. Last night they came   seeking shelter from the cold and snow, sleeping on the floor in front of the genial fire for warmth. I wanted to hold my nose for the whole room smelled of bear grease. I wonder what good they think rubbing bear grease on their skin would do?

After they had left, Christian told me that Thomas Chalkly (a minister who came to the New World on the *Mary Hope*), has spent some time with the Conestoga Indians and preached to them. Also, Quaker William Penn treated the Indians with great respect, making agreements with them for settlements on their territories, and by so doing securing their cooperation and approval. I do hope it stays that way and that the whites will never betray their trust.

The snow tapered off at mid-forenoon and the wind died down. Now tonight it's much milder again and the eaves are dripping.

✍

November 3: The weather is sunny and much warmer again. On Sunday we had church services again in the *stube*, and I was able to learn more about what Christ has done for us on the cross and also about redemption from the curse of sin. Tonight Grosdaudy Hans kindly explained some of the things that I found hard to understand—making them seem so much clearer. I will copy down some things I learned, lest I forget them: The Lord is not willing that any should perish, but wants all to come to repentance and acknowledgement of the truth. Behold, even now the Saviour is knocking on my heart's door – one of His wandering sheep. He says, "Him that cometh unto Me I will in no wise cast out." Tears flowed down over my cheeks as I asked Him to take over my life. Some of the tears were for my mother, too. She would have loved these precious truths, too, had she understood them better.

This afternoon Anna was making stewed dumplings in the big kettle on the raised hearth in the *küche*, and sent me to the cellar for a panful of apples to bake in the iron dutch oven. I took little Anna along, for she's becoming very fond of me and wants to toddle after me wherever I go. The cellar is a large arched one, filled with garden goodies. I was astonished at the sight of the 50 gallon barrels of cider! Also, lots of apples, cabbages, turnips, and carrots. The rainfall must have been ample to yield such a bounteous harvest. Cured meats hung from a pole through two rings in the ceiling. Butter-filled pots stood on a shelf. Such bounteous provisions!

It is evening now and Anna is filling the iron betty-lamp on the candlestand. She fills it from a long-spouted copper can with melted lard. Little Anna just now came running to me with her cornhusk doll, wanting to be held. The boys are at the *stube* table, reciting their lessons. Even little Abraham recites after his brothers. Anna approves of me writing in my copybook—I think she may even be a bit envious. I'm beginning to dearly love this family and wish I could stay. But since I'm learning to place my trust in the Most High as Anna tells me to, I want to say, "Thy will be done."

November 7: This morning Uncle Hendrick arrived by horseback at the Herr's house, and I was made to say a tearful goodbye to my adopted family. It was even more heart-wrenching than saying goodbye to Hannah Keith. At that time I had never thought I could become so attached to this family so soon. Anna, too, had tears in her eyes when she bade me goodbye, and said

she hopes I'll be back someday. Christian wished me the Lord's blessings, and Grosdaudy Hans clasped my hand and said he hoped I would stay close to God and walk the narrow way. The children clamored around me—baby Anna clung to my skirts and cried when I had to go. I wondered (tearfully) if I would ever see them again, for goodbyes even here on this earth are often final.

It's evening now and I am utterly weary. Uncle Hendrick and I were riding through the woods on a barely discernable trail most of the day, not even stopping to make a fire at noon to cook dinner. I wonder if he is always such a man of few words, or if it's because he was so disappointed or displeased that Mother isn't along. He's not at all like I remember my father to be. He seemed to be in a great hurry—if he has a reason for his haste he didn't mention it. Perhaps it is because (though it was mild and sunny today) it is the time of year when another cold snap and snowstorm could head our way anytime. We're heading for his cabin in the woods quite a ways from here, and I suppose he's anxious to put out his trapline. I won't take up space to write down my fears, but somehow, I don't think Uncle is a very trustworthy man. If only he'd be more friendly and sociable. There's nothing but a feeling of dread for the months ahead, living alone in the middle of the forest with him. As we traveled through thickening woods and brush, my thoughts dwelt on strange fears and foreboding. What if he's not my uncle at all, but instead some other unscrupulous fellow kidnapping me? For the thousandth time I wished I'd have begged to stay with the Herrs, or even refused to go for any reason.

How I cling to my new-found faith now. Surely God will take care of me. Uncle has built a fire and is roasting rabbit meat on a stick. Ugh! Half raw meat, instead of well-cooked and bubbling in brown gravy. Oh well, I'm too exhausted to eat anything tonight anyway.

When I took my copybook and quill out of my satchel, Uncle asked me what I'm writing. When I told him about my journal, he clearly seemed disgusted with such foolishness. At least he didn't tell me to throw it in the creek. Perhaps writing in my copybook will help to dispel the loneliness, silences, and stark bareness of Penn's Woods.

✍

November 8: It's evening again and I am almost too weary to keep my eyes open. I managed to eat a few bites of roast rabbit last night, then rolled into my blanket and slept the sleep of exhaustion. In his bedroll on the other side of the fire, Uncle snored so loudly that it half-woke me time and again.

We traveled even further today than yesterday. I think we must soon be in the depths of the wilderness. The skies were gray and dreary both days, matching my spirits. I felt utterly lonely tonight, wishing that Uncle would at least talk. He merely grunts in reply when I say something. It makes me thankful for my copybook and my good supply of black walnut ink. When I took up my quill pen and began to write, he did speak though. He said with a snort of derision, "What a waste of time! Do you think the Indians will care for a copybook when they seek your scalp? Do you think it will save your life?"

"What!" I cried fearfully. "I thought the Indians were friendly!"

He merely shrugged his shoulders, saying, "The friendly Conestogas aren't the only red men about. There's the Maryland Indians, the Paxtons, and perhaps even some Shawnees." He stopped abruptly then, as if he wished he hadn't said it, and rolled himself into his bedroll. I am too weary to feel any fear, though; only dread and a feeling of foreboding. I take solace in prayer, trusting in the living God as the Herrs taught me.

Time to turn in, for the fire embers are dying down, making it hard for me to see to write. I hope I'll be able to sleep well in spite of Uncle's snoring.

✍

November 9: It is evening and I am again sitting near a campfire, but in quite a different setting than in my last entry. I feel as if I could go mad with fear and dread. This morning as Uncle and I started off for yet another day's journey, I suddenly heard a whoop, then three painted Indians suddenly came out of the thickets. An arrow whizzed through the air and Uncle fell from the horse. Rough hands seized me and the next thing I knew I was being dragged through the woods by my hair. If I hadn't had the long drawstrings of my satchel around my neck, it, along with my copybook surely would have been left behind. The Indians do not seem to care that I am writing, but they do stare at me in something like amazement. Perhaps they think it is something like magic.

The sight of them, and the fear and dismay nauseates me. They tried to force me to eat some bear meat they roasted over the fire, but I just gagged. O God, out of the depths of my heart I cry for help.

✍

November 10: I do not want to lose track of the days. My second day of traveling with the Indians is drawing to a close. Today I thought of doing something to leave a trail, to guide someone trying to rescue me. Until I realized that no one knows where I am and that I was captured. No one, but Uncle, and he is gone. The Indians would never have left him just half dead. I had no affection for him, but still my tears flow. O Mother, Mother, I am sinking in utter despair! Oh Hannah Keith! Oh Anna and Christian Herr! Oh Grosdaudy Hans! Oh God, help me! At night they tie me up with thongs of buffalo rope. All day I must walk, walk, walk. My feet are blistered, scratched, and bleeding. The sun doesn't shine and the weather is wet, very damp, and dismal. At times a foggy drizzle obscures our path. But always, in front of me and behind, the sight of those repulsive redskins. They take turns riding, but I must walk. They make brush beds for themselves to sleep on, but I sleep on the rocky ground. But my heart is thankful that they ignore me most of the time. How long shall I be able to endure the strain? Ahead looms another day of wearisome walking through the wilderness, up hills, down into valleys, along streams, through deep ravines. Not knowing what lies ahead makes me shudder. Are they taking me to their village or wherever they live, to torture me or perhaps even to force me to be the wife or squaw of a warrior?

One of them swiped from me the precious beads Marquis had given me on the ship and that I wanted to save as a remembrance of him. I wouldn't have worn them for the Herrs don't approve of jewelry, but still, I cherished them. Worse yet, one of them came close to me and lifted a strand of my hair and said something to the others. They nodded and laughed, talking among themselves. A pang swept through me—I had just about forgotten that I have copper-colored hair, for the Herrs have no mirrors. The Indians must be fascinated by red hair.

But how can I sit here, calmly writing, not knowing the terrors that might lie ahead? Maybe because writing about it seems to calm me somewhat. I am trying to become fully resigned to my fate.

✍

O horrors! Susie thought, as she closed the book for the evening. *Captured by the Indians. What will happen to poor Dorothea Marguerite now. It's too bad her uncle couldn't have been different—a family man with a homestead like Christian Herr, for example. She'd have been better off staying with Hannah Keith. I don't know if I can wait until tomorrow night to find out more.*

But she did, for it was past 9 o'clock and Dannie was banking the fire for the night. She would have to endure the suspense.

6

Lost in the Woods

Susie was so engrossed in the story, that she thought about it all the next day as she did her school work and then walked home. She tingled with Dorothea Marguerite's anxiety and fear, as she was forced to travel with the Indians. After the choring was finished, when she finally was able to start reading again, she was soon completely wrapped up in the book.

November 11: Today my spirits lifted somewhat, for the Lord seemed very close. I rememberd a verse that Christian Herr read at the last church service: "Though He slay me, yet will I trust in Him." I couldn't fathom what it meant, at the time, but now I think I do. God sees even the little sparrows that fall.

I am too tired to write much tonight. The Indians seem restless and uneasy, as if they're expecting some danger ahead. I always sleep fully clothed and with the drawstrings of my satchel over my shoulder. Yet how foolish it is to cling to one's belongings when you never know how soon you'll wake up in eternity.

✍

November 12: How still and peaceful the woods are! Birds are twittering in the treetops and a few leaves float lazily down in a shaft of weak sunlight filtering through the trees. I feel a numbness creeping through my being, but it is not from the cold, for it is still mild. Am I dreaming, or am I really all alone in the depths of Penn's Woods, where the fierce wild beasts may roam? Oh, what would Mother say! How is it that I feel no panic— not even fear? I think it's because it is so sweet to me to no longer be in the hands of the redskins that I am numb to the other dangers. Yet the realization is there somewhere, for I find myself wishing that I could have gone with my mother to the bosom of the ocean. The prospect of starvation, being torn by wild beasts, or captured again by the Indians are not very alluring. Was it really just this morning that it happened?

We were done with breakfast and had just put out the fire, ready to start off on our day's journey. The Indians seemed to sense danger nearby, but I was totally unprepared for the savage cries and arrows and tomahawks flying as another band of Indians descended upon us. I ducked into the woods, scrambling behind a dense thicket, and then ran blindly— dodging the brambles, jumping over rocks, and crawling underneath pines and hemlocks. I ran until I was so winded that

I had to stop and catch my breath. Then I blindly ran on, not knowing in which direction I was going, for the skies were gray with clouds. I kept on running as long as I could, then walked the rest of the day. Now darkness is approaching and I must find shelter for the night, but I am too exhausted to take another step.

I don't believe those Indian enemies were interested in a captive white girl, for they could easily have trailed me and caught me if they'd have had a mind to. They were probably out for revenge on a rival tribe and their victory satisfied them. How is it that I no longer feel any fear or dread in my perilous situation? Perhaps it's the knowledge that God delivered me from the hands of the Indians, and He can take care of and deliver me now from the beasts and starvation if it is His will. I remember Christian Herr reading a Bible story of one named Daniel who was thrown into a den of lions. God closed the lions' mouths and he was not harmed. What a miracle! I pray that He will miraculously save me also.

✍

November 13: Last night I found shelter in a big hollow log. I rolled a big rock against one end and barricaded the other end with dried leaves and branches, pulling them in after me. When I heard the howling of a wolf in the distance, I trembled so violently that I thought the log might roll over. But it came no closer, and soon the sleep of exhaustion overtook me. After I had slept half the night in the log, I was awakened by sniffing sounds outside. I hardly dared to breathe, knowing a wild creature was there, and I prayed earnestly and fervently. God heard my cry and the beast finally wandered away. This morning there was abundant sunshine, which greatly cheered me. I believe I am quite a ways south and west of the Herr's home, so I will try to travel toward the northeast. May God guide my footsteps and lead me straight back to them, for I know they would not turn me away homeless. He will have to protect me

from the wild creatures too, and provide me with manna from Heaven.

☙

November 14: I feel as if I should write a journal entry everyday, so I can keep track of the days. This morning the air was quite nippy, so I got the shawl Hannah Keith gave me out of my satchel, and wound it around my cloak. The sun had disappeared behind gray clouds and I do believe it is going to snow soon.

After spending an increasingly uncomfortable night in a rocky crevice, my spirits were very low this morning, and I wasted a good hour's time crying. I have had very little to eat since I've been alone—just some tasteless persimmons, some unpalatable roots, and a few dried berries. But still, I do not feel as weak and sick as I did on the big ship coming over. I have seen and heard no more of any Indians, perhaps they've all left for their winter dwelling places. I wish I could fly away on a great white cloud, up to the dwelling place of the Most High, and be at rest.

✍

November 15: Once again I sit by a crackling campfire tonight, and bask in its glow of warmth. It's still hard for me to comprehend. Maybe I am dreaming. Last evening as the shadows deepened in the forest, I wearily trudged through the thickets, seeking shelter from the wind and flurrying snow. I was so weak that I tripped over roots and stones, and snagged my hair on the brambles that overhung the way, but I was too tired to care. I blundered on, feeling on the point of collapse. Then a stout branch wedged between two rocks tripped me, and I fell headlong to the ground. In my weakened condition it was all too much for me and I sank down on a log and buried my head in my arms, and was wracked with great, silent shuddering sobs. The thought of the long black night ahead filled me with a dread as black as the night itself.

After I was so cried out that I felt I could cry no more, I suddenly straightened up. Was that a gleam of light I saw in the distance? Immediately I was not as tired as I had thought. Disregarding the thickets between us, I straightaway pressed toward the glimmer ahead. It was a campfire, and someone must have just then added more wood, for the flames leapt upward. And then I heard the low whinny of a horse. A sudden glad hope lent wings to my feet and I pressed forward. But then a new thought suddenly filled me with panic and stopped me in my tracks. What if it was a band of Indians? Still, I warily and cautiously

proceeded, intending to retreat the moment I actually saw them.
Trying to move as silently as an Indian, I crept forward. As I
rounded a thicket, the fire came into my line of vision and I gave
a gasp. A man with his back to me, bent over the fire, securing a
piece of meat on a skewer. I stood there, transfixed for a moment. The aroma of the meat sizzling over the fire filled me with
longing and set my stomach to gnawing and my mouth to water-
ing. But when he lifted his head I quickly stepped back into the

shadows, for I had no way of knowing whether he was a friend or foe, trustworthy or unscrupulous. In that same instant, the man dropped his meat, grabbed his rifle, and leapt to his feet. I quickly sank down behind a thicket and began to creep away. Then a twig cracked sharply behind me and I felt myself being grabbed by the arm and jerked into the firelight. I cowered there in fear and trembling, not knowing what would come next.

The man gave a long, low whistle of astonishment. Gathering courage, I lifted my head and saw that it was a young man (not an Indian) gazing at me in speechless wonder. He did not look like a criminal, rather, there was an appealing expression of good-hearted honesty on his frank, open features.

"Wh-where do you hail from, Little Redhead?" he finally managed to stammer. "I never expected to find . . ."

After a long moment of silence, I felt so unnerved that I burst into tears.

"There now, I didn't mean to frighten you." The young man seemed eager to make amends.

"Warm yourself by the fire and help yourself to a piece of meat. You look like you could use some sustenance." He kindly handed me a skewer, which was a green stick with a still sizzling chunk of meat on the end of it. My fear of the man had flown and I needed no second invitation, being ravenous past caring. I huddled by the fire, relishing the juicy, browned morsel of meat, and savoring the warmth of the glowing embers.

"My name is Jethro Arden," he ventured after another long wondering pause. "What's yours and how did you get lost in this great forest?" He seemed so friendly and sincere that I suddenly found myself telling him everything—the passage on the ship, my mother's death, Hannah Keith, Scar Face, staying with the Herrs and my wish to return to them, my uncle, and of being captured by the Indians.

Jethro gave another long, low whistle, exclaiming, "My, you've been through a lot. How did you expect to get out of your predicament without any provisions and not even a gun?"

"I prayed," I said shyly. "The Herrs told me to ask God for His protection. I guess I was beginning to feel, though, that it might be His will for me to perish in the wilderness."

"I'll do everything in my power to prevent that," Jethro said fervently. "I think I can find my way to the Herr's homestead. I believe I've heard of Hans and Christian Herr. Aren't they the ones that built a big stone house which they use for having church services, too? Peter Bazallion has spoken of them several times."

I nodded. "But I don't want to spoil your plans. If you're just heading that way on account of me . . ."

But Jethro cut me off. "Think nothing of it," he protested. "I'm a trapper, and have a cabin about 20 miles south of here. I was on my way there, but I can come and go as I please. If the snows hold off I can get you home to the Herrs and return to my trapline in record time. My horse Penny is as faithful and dependable as they come. You can ride Barney, my pack horse, and before another week rolls around you should be safe and sound with the Herrs. But say, you look about all done in! Forgive me . . . here's a bedroll for you. Just make yourself comfortable by the fire." He unrolled the bedroll and motioned me to it.

I knew it must be his own, but I was too tired to care. Rolled up in its warmth, tears insisted on filling my eyes. I was thinking, God and His provisions are good. The Indians seem to have left these parts and all is peaceful. My last waking thoughts were of wondering why such a likeable young man only 25 years of age, as he told me, would choose a life of solitude in the woods. He seems to be a man of character and integrity as far as I can tell. Perhaps it's his love of the outdoors, and hunting and trapping that lures him.

The next thing I knew it was morning and Jethro had built up the fire and was kneeling beside it with a skewered chunk of meat sizzling over it, sending a wonderful aroma wafting over to me. I lifted up on one elbow watching as he roasted the meat.

"Good morning," I greeted him. "Isn't it amazing how meat puts the strength back into one's trembling bones and even the aroma of it can lift one's spirits and hearten a person!"

"Good morning, Little Redhead." His eyes lit up in greeting. "I was beginning to wonder if you were going to sleep until noon." He laid a delectable looking piece of meat on a tin plate and skewered another piece on a green twig.

"I might have if I hadn't smelled the meat. I still feel half starved, absolutely ravenous. I hope I don't eat up all your provisions, though."

"Never fear. I have plenty and there's plenty of game in the woods. Set to and eat hearty. You'll need your strength for traveling."

After breakfast was over, I went to the stream to wash my face and hands in the icy cold water. The sun was lighting up the eastern sky with a faint pink glow. The snow clouds had disappeared and it looked to be clear weather ahead. A pair of chickadees flitted cheekily through the bushes and a turkey hen scuttled through the underbrush. My outlook was so very different from the day before that I felt I could sing a song of praise. Before I had felt so helpless and close to perishing, but now there's a trustworthy trapper to take me back to the Herrs. I feel so much more comfortable with Jethro than I felt with my uncle. My spirits had sunk quite low just thinking about spending several years with him in the wilderness. Now I have something to look forward to—going back to live with sweet-natured Anna Herr's family! God be thanked!

I'll try to make an occasional trip to Philadelphia too, to visit Hannah Keith, but I don't think I'll go back to permanently living with her and her abundance of riches, even with all her kindness. I'm not used to such elegant surroundings, and don't think I'd like to be a lady of leisure. The Herrs feel that plainness, thrift, and simplicity are a part of godly living. I remember Christian reading aloud a Bible verse: "Whosoever among you wants to be the greatest, let him be the servant of all." They live clean and work hard, and I want to be like that, too. Time to lay this aside, for the firelight is dying down and darkness steals softly through the woods. Jethro sits gazing meditatively into the fire, glancing at me every now and then. Sometimes I wish I could read his thoughts. If he's disgusted about having to escort me back to the Herrs, he surely doesn't show it. I'd like to ask him if he's a follower of Christ, maybe even an Anabaptist, but I haven't the courage yet.

I thank the Lord for sending him to me, to save me from perishing in the woods. From the bottom of my heart I thank Him for His care and provisions.

✍

Well! thought Susie. *So that's the trapper who is going to help her find her way back to the Herrs. He sure seems like a nice, decent fellow. Lucky for Dorothea Marguerite!* She put the marker into the book and laid it on the shelf. Tomorrow night couldn't come too soon for her.

7

Rescued By a Trapper

The next evening Susie told Dannie the story of Dorothea Marguerite as they fed the calves, then bedded them. To her surprise he was beginning to sound interested, too. "I'm surprised the Indians let the girl get away," he said. "I don't believe that would've happened very often."

"Maybe not," Susie replied. "But still, our teacher told us that quite a few white youngsters had been captured by the Indians. After the French and Indian War was over, they were released and allowed to return to their parents."

"I know, but that was different," Dannie pointed out. "The government made them return the captives. It was the law."

"Ya well, Dorothea Marguerite's escape might have been nothing less than a miracle," Susie declared. "Miracles can happen anytime."

Dannie chuckled. "I guess I'll have to read that story too, sometime. You sure seem smitten by it. Hand it over when you're done."

Back in the house, Susie took down her book and sank into the rocker, propping her feet on the oven door for warmth, and began to read.

✍

November 16: This morning when I awoke, the sky was just heralding the approach of dawn. On the other side of the fire, Jethro was still rolled up in his blanket, his back to the fire. A chilly breeze was whistling through the trees, but I was cozy warm inside my bedroll. A cock pheasant crowed from the thickets and Jethro sat up and stretched his arms to the sky, flexing his broad, powerful-looking shoulders. I saw him raise his eyes to the treetops and then an amused smile flitted across his features. A bushy-tailed squirrel was running back and forth on a branch about 15 feet above, scolding and chirping mightily. I don't think Jethro was aware of the fact that I was awake. For the first time I had an uninterrupted look at my rescuer's face, without having to look away quickly when he felt my gaze and returned it. I noticed that his brows were well-shaped, his eyes brown and set well apart. His face is likeable, full of "character "and entirely masculine.

I wondered if perhaps he has a sweetheart or a mother or sister back home waiting for him, and praying for him. I never had a brother and I found myself wishing he were mine. He certainly has treated me as finely as any young man would treat his sister, and I feel entirely safe with him. The first night after he had found me, I hoped that he would sleep somewhere out of sight but still within calling distance. But when I heard a pack of wolves howling too close for comfort, I knew that would not be practical nor wise. He needed the fire, too, for protection, and he had to keep it going. He is not the kind of man that would take advantage of a girl in her helpless dependence upon him for care and protection, though, thank God.

Jethro soon noticed that I was awake, and his cheery, "Good morning, Little Redhead," greeted me and I jumped up to help with the breakfast. Jethro laid some dry twigs on the fire, and the embers soon took hold of them and shot up in bright wavering flames. The coffee was soon bubbling in the pot and a trout was sizzling over the fire. I thought longingly of the pancakes and maple syrup we'd had at the Herrs, but after having felt the pangs of starvation, I was extremely grateful for our provisions. After our appetites had been satisfied, we sat awhile in companionable silence. Jethro sat staring into the dancing flames while he finished his coffee. He kept glancing at me, and then a mischievous smile flitted across his face, which was immediately replaced by a thoughtful look.

"I've been traipsing through the heart of Penn's Woods for nearly 7 years now," he told me. "Both of my parents died during a flu epidemic when I was 10 years old. I went to live with my uncle and aunt. My uncle died when I was 18 and my aunt went to live with an elderly neighbor couple. I knew then that my chance had come to come across to the New World. I've never been sorry I came or wished for another occupation, for I love the woodlands and the outdoor life. In this wide new land there were mountains of fantastic beauty and magnificent forests full of wild game. There were scenic rivers and winding streams full of fish and furs ready to be caught. There's nothing comparable to outdoor living, under trees mighty and luxuriant, and on soil bursting with fertility. Someday I plan to own a homestead; to clear off the trees, till the soil and raise fine crops. I've been happy and free, but until now, I never realized what I was missing—the congenial companionship of another human. I wish . . ."

But I never found out what Jethro wished, for he suddenly clammed up and resolutely jumped to his feet to pack up the gear for the day's journey. He said, "Forgive me, Little Redhead, for speaking improperly. I certainly will do everything in my power to get you safely back to the Herrs." Then he spoke not another word as we rode through the forest, not until we stopped to make camp to cook dinner at high noon. I was pondering his words all the while, wondering why he said, "forgive me." Had he been contemplating kidnapping me and taking me to his cabin, so he could have companionship in the long winter ahead? But, of course not! His "I wish" could have meant, though, "I wish we had time to get better acquainted," or "I wish we didn't have to live miles and miles apart." With each plod of the horses' hooves, my heart was chanting those very wishes, too, for I've never met a nicer nor more sensible young man than Jethro. But it will never do to jump to conclusions. For, perhaps his "I wish" had meant, "I wish I didn't have to take the time to escort you to the Herrs." So I turned my thoughts to anticipating our arrival there, and to thinking about the Heavenly Father they taught me to trust. I remember Anna kindly reminding me, before I started off with Uncle Hendrick, that all things work together for good for God's children who are called according to His purpose.

By mid-afternoon I was weary and chilled to the bone and very saddle sore with a cramping ache in my tailbone, as we rode through a stand of pines, spruce, firs, and thickets of berry bushes. There was no trail. I was amazed that Jethro was able to find his way. Even when the sun is not out to guide him, he seems to know, probably by the landmarks. There are hillsides and ravines, brooks and streams. He must be quite as skilled and knowledgeable in woodlore as the Indians. Speaking of Indians, we haven't seen a trace of them since the battle that gave me my freedom. Perhaps they killed each other, one and all. I wouldn't mind the friendly Conestogas, I think I'd feel safer with them nearby, especially if there would be other tribes in the vicinity.

When Jethro caught on to how chilly and weary I was of riding, he suggested that I could walk for awhile instead. That warmed me up considerably and relieved the soreness in my tail-bone. It slowed our pace, but it couldn't be helped. I was weary of riding, too, when I was with Uncle, but I didn't think about it as much, because of my other concerns.

The stars are coming out now and the bare trees are swaying in the breeze. It's so comforting to sit by a crackling fire instead of being alone in a night black as the pit, with no shelter from wild beasts. I would try not to think of the bears, panthers, and wolves prowling out there, but I could never put it out of my mind.

Oh, Heavenly Father, thank you again for sending Jethro my way to rescue me. Thank you for a cheerful fire and the savory aroma of meat roasting over it. Help us to make it safely to the Herrs.

November 17: I awoke again at dawn this morning, watching the sunrise thrust aside night's somber curtains, revealing a sky overcast with gray slated clouds. I so hoped it wouldn't rain or snow, which would hinder us getting to the Herrs. When Jethro unrolled from his blanket, with his usual, "Good morning, Redhead," he was in a cheerful mood. He must be the type of person that is at his best in the morning, for by evening he is tired and not as alert. He whistled as he chopped up some dry branches with his hatchet and piled sticks on the fire, and then put coffee in the pot. Neither of us had an inkling of a tragedy ahead.

Our spirits were high as we, refreshed from our night's sleep, started on our day's journey. Ragged wisps of clouds chased across the sky's gray, and a blustery wind made me pull my shawl tightly around my cloak. From now on, when travelling I carry my satchel inside my cloak so that my hands are free. Jethro's horse stepped sprightly along, and my Barney followed obediently after him. Jethro was in a talkative mood; he is knowledgeable about a good many things and very interesting. The morn-

ing sped by as if on wings, and before I realized it, noon-time was upon us. By then the weather had moderated a bit and we decided not to take the time to make a fire. Cold vittles would have to do us. It would save us time and we could be on our way sooner.

After we had finished the meal, Jethro got the horses ready and I sat down on a stump, waiting to mount my ride. Suddenly, I heard a twig snap behind me and saw a look of terror leap into Jethro's eyes. He had set his rifle against a tree on the other side of the horses, but his hatchet was at his belt. Fast as lightning he grabbed up his weapon, swung it up over his head and came rushing straight at me—or so it seemed. Before I could jump out of the way or even duck, Jethro was beside me, knocking me out of danger's way. I heard a crunching blow and in that same instant a heavy body crashed to the earth right beside me. A furry, rank-smelling whirlwind thrashed beside me and I covered my head with my hands. I heard another crunching blow and then a fearsome roar. Blood splayed over me as I heard an agonized scream. There was a flailing and thrashing as the beast rolled away from me, then got up on its hind legs. I had a glimpse of a huge bear, its jaws wide open baring ferocious teeth, and black eyes glittering with rage. I covered my eyes again, sure that the bear would be upon me in a second. Suddenly there was the mighty boom of the rifle; it seemed to shake the ground underneath me. The bear crumpled to the ground. The rifle cracked again and the bear lay still.

I laid there for a moment, dazed and trembling, then Jethro was bending over me, his face ashen. "Are you hurt, Little Redhead?" he said as his voice quivered. "That bear was coming straight for you, his mouth wide open and his paws outspread. If I'd have gone for my gun first, he'd have had you. I can't bear to think what would have happened if I'd have missed that first swing at his head. Even so, he still had plenty of fight left in him." Jethro suddenly swayed and reached out an arm to steady himself.

"Jethro! You're hurt!" I cried in alarm, noticing for the first time that his shirt sleeve was ripped from seam to seam, baring his sinewy, blood-spattered arm. His pant leg was ripped, too, revealing an ugly bloody gash.

"I'll be all right." He tried to steady his voice. "Just give me a few minutes," he said as he lowered his head nearly to his knees.

"I'll get you some water." I hurried to the nearby brook with the coffee tin, skirting the black carcass of the bear by a wide margin. I looked warily around, fearing that the bear might have a mate somewhere, ready to rush out at me. I dipped my handkerchief into the brook and also filled the cup. "Please God," I whispered, "help Jethro. Heal his wounds. I'd never get back to the Herrs without him."

By the time I had returned with the water, Jethro's color had come back and he was looking better. "Thank goodness the bleeding has stopped," he said. "It would be good to bind up the wounds in clean rags, though, and that's just what we haven't got." He scrubbed away at the splattered blood on his arm and face with the wet handkerchief. "If you will be so good to bring me other clothes from my pack, I'll try to make myself more presentable. This shirt is in shreds."

"The horses!" I cried out in dismay. "They're gone! Now we're stranded, surely!"

Jethro didn't seem alarmed. "I don't blame them for clearing out. They'll come when I whistle, but not until we move away from Mr. Bruin."

Luckily, the pack with his extra clothes had fallen off and I went to retrieve it. As I bent over, my top petticoat showed underneath my skirt and I got a sudden inspiration. Jethro would have something after all to bind up his wounds. I ripped off a wide strip and carried it and the clothes to him.

"Very thoughtful of you, thank you," was his grateful response. "That should help to heal these wounds in a trice." Together we cleaned the wounds as best as we could and wrapped the petticoat strips around them. I turned my back as he donned his other clothes, resolving to try and mend the torn ones somehow.

"I can't understand what instigated that attack. It's a puzzle to me," Jethro remarked. "I've been a woodsman for years and I've never heard of a bear tackling anyone like that, especially if they weren't wounded, cornered, or protecting cubs. There was no cause or reason that I can see." He bent to take a closer look at the bear, then exclaimed, "That's it! Just look! There's part of a broken arrow deeply imbedded in the bear's side! It's protruding from an old wound. It could've been there for quite awhile and now became infected. The bear was probably sick from the festering wound and crazed with pain."

"Thank God he's dead." I shuddered at the thought of his coming at me like that.

Gritting his teeth from the pain, Jethro limped a good distance away from the bear, then, with two fingers in his mouth, gave forth a shrill whistle that brought Penny and Barney ambling back to him. We had decided that since Jethro wasn't feeling up to skinning the bear, we would let the carcass lay, though it was a pity to just let it rot. So, it was that a short time later we were on our way again, but going at a slower pace. I pitied Jethro when I saw the beads of sweat come out on his forehead. He had risked his life for me. He could have gone for his gun and shot the bear, but he chose to put himself in danger to protect and save my life.

Tonight I had to gather the firewood and cook the supper alone. Jethro is curled up in his blanket sleeping. It gives me an "alone" feeling. I must keep the fire going and watch over him. The stars are twinkling in the black sky and a screech owl's quavering hoot sounds from the trees. It sounds scary and eerie, but I'd rather hear an owl's call than wolves howling. A while ago, I saw a pair of yellow eyes shining out of the darkness, then silently they disappeared. Tonight is one night that I long for four solid walls around us and a roof overhead. Oh God, please keep us from danger and harm.

✍

November 19: We've had two more days of traveling, which was slow going and painful for Jethro. He says there's a cabin just ahead, which we'll possibly reach tomorrow and then we'll stay there until his wounds are healed. I sure would enjoy a good rest, too, and the safety of a cabin. I haven't had a good night's sleep since Jethro was hurt, and it's telling on me. I feel jumpy and short-tempered and Jethro's face looks grim and lined. He doesn't complain, but he doesn't look well.

I often think back to when Mother and I lived alone in our humble little dwelling. We were poor, but we were happy.

If only we hadn't left it. If only we could have foreseen that Mother wouldn't survive the journey and that I would end up in these terrible dangers in Penn's Woods. But I want to trust in the living God. Anna Herr told me that He plans our lives and that we dare not question His dealings with us. Someday we'll understand.

✍

The clock had struck nine bells some time ago, so Susie reluctantly placed a marker in her book and placed it on the shelf. "Attacked by a bear!" she exclaimed. "That was a close call! What awful terrors and unexpected dangers there were in Penn's Woods in those days."

When Dannie made no reply, she quickly glanced at him. His head was nodding and his book had slid out of his hand and was ready to fall to the floor. Mischievously, Susie got a kernel of popcorn and snapped it at Dannie. It hit him on the arm and he jerked instantly awake.

"I thought for sure it was an arrowhead, coming my way," he joked good-naturedly. "Better watch out if you don't want to hear an Indian war whoop!"

8

Indians to the Rescue

S usie squirted Windex on the window above the sink and rubbed it with a paper towel. *In just one more week Steven, Annie, and little Suzanne will be home,* she thought happily. *I can't wait to scoop my little namesake up into my arms again. Being on our own is fun for Dannie and me, but handing back the responsibilities to them will be a relief.* She put the cleaning supplies into the closet, then hurried into her chore clothes and boots. As soon as the work was done, she put milk on the stove to heat for cocoa, then curled up on the rocker to resume her story.

November 20: What a good and secure feeling it is to
be inside a sturdy cabin with a cheerful fire blazing on the hearth,
warming every corner of the room. Such a surprise it was to learn
that this was Uncle Hendrick's cabin! His name was carved into
the wood above the mantle. He will never again need the provisions he has here, so we know it's all right to help ourselves.
There's plenty of hay for the horses in the stable, and there are

pumpkins, squash, dried beans, and onions in the loft, cabbages and turnips in the cellar, and plenty of cornmeal in the larder. There's also a winter's supply of firewood stacked on both sides of the door.

How cozy it would all seem if it weren't for Jethro's condition. He has a raging fever and his wounds are festering. He's sleeping in Uncle's bed now, but sometimes I hear him moaning. If only I could do something to make him feel better. I wondered, should I sponge his hot forehead with cold water, or would that be too forward of me? Tonight I felt almost glad to get out of the cabin when I went to feed the horses. They were very glad to see me, greeting me with low, throaty whinnies and stamping their feet and trying to nuzzle me with their velvety noses. Of course, it was the feed that made them so eager. I'm very thankful that Uncle Hendrick put up plenty of hay, corn, and winter provisions. Maybe he wasn't such a bad sort after all—could be I just hadn't gotten to know him yet.

When I went back to the cabin, Jethro was still moaning. I felt I must do something, so I grabbed the wooden bucket on the bench and went out to the spring flowing from the rocks at the edge of the clearing. The western sky was a glow of red sunset, and I paused to admire the beauty of it and thought of that Wonderful Place beyond the sunset, where there is no sickness or pain. From a blackberry bramble, English sparrows twittered and hopped from twig to twig. It all seemed so peaceful and lovely until I heard a lone howl from a far ridge. Remembering the bear and all the other dangers, I shiveringly hurried back to the cabin. Taking down the dipper on the hook above the rickety little table, I poured cold water over the dish rag. Summoning all my courage, I took it to my feverish patient and laid it on his brow. I think it made him feel better for awhile, for he gave me a slight smile and ceased his tossing and turning, and soon afterward he fell asleep.

I have a batch of cornmeal mush bubbling in the iron kettle over the fire that I must not forget to stir every now and then. I feel so tired and worn out that I plan to crawl into my bed right after supper. I've rigged up a makeshift bed in a corner—it's actually just a bearskin covered with my shawl, but it will sleep like royalty, compared to crawling into a hollow log. I'm praying to God to heal Jethro speedily and to give him a good night's sleep.

✍

November 21: The ground was covered with a light dusting of snow this morning when I went to the spring for a bucket of water. At the edges of the pool there was thin ice which I had to break before I could dip up the ice cold water. I saw lots of tracks from deer, raccoon, pheasant, rabbits, and mice. The trees stand silent and leafless, like tall sentinels reaching their arms to the sky. I'm glad the trees are bare, or else I might be afraid to go to the spring in the early morning, for a panther might be concealed in the branches waiting to pounce down on me.

✍

Jethro's condition wasn't much better this morning. I tried to feed him some thinned corn mush, but I don't think he took more than half a teaspoonful. He had a very restless night, but is lying quietly now—perhaps sleeping. I can't begin to write how anxious I am about him. If he should die . . . I . . . I'd never find my way back to the Herrs. I'd be stranded here in this cabin until my provisions were gone and then I'd have to venture forth alone, that is, if the Indians hadn't found me by then.

I'm cooking a stew made of turnips, dried beans, and dried venison in the big iron kettle over the fire. Some of that bear meat we left laying in the woods would taste good roasted over the fire. I wonder if Jethro will ever feel well enough again to go hunting for fresh meat? I'm trusting in God's help, and exceedingly thankful for Uncle Hendrick's provisions.

✍

November 22: This morning I decided it was high time to do some washing of clothes, even though Jethro wasn't any better. I knew I couldn't wash everything at once, for we needed things to wear, too. My good intentions caused a near calamity though, and by it brought us the help of a friend. There was a strong northwest wind whistling through the trees and around the corner of the cabin. I made repeated trips to the spring with my bucket and filled the iron kettle with water. Then I stirred up the fire and piled a great stack of fire-wood on it, never realizing how I was endangering ourselves by doing so. The wind was blowing harder than ever and the fire roared to life. The flames licked up the chimney with a roar and heated my wash water in a jiffy. It seemed like just a few moments later, when I stepped outside to get another bucket of water from the spring for rinsing, when my heart gave a lurch of fear.

The stable roof was on fire! A spark from the chimney must have ignited it! With a desperate shriek, I grabbed the bucket and ran for the spring. If only I could splash enough water on it before it could take a real hold! For although the flame was small now, in this wind it wouldn't take long. My mind was reeling, wondering if it would be best to lead out the horses first. If there wasn't time to save the stable, maybe the horses could at least be saved. I ran with the full bucket, as fast as my strength allowed me, trying not to spill any of the water. Sobs tore at my throat as I saw the flame creep slowly up the side of the roof. Suddenly, my eye caught a movement at the edge of the clearing. With a powerful leap, a lone figure bounded over to me, grabbed the bucket, and with a mighty heave doused the fire with the water. I could only stand and stare as he ran to the spring for another bucketful and splashed water over the roof again, even though the fire appeared to be out. It was an Indian lad dressed in fringed buckskin. Smiling, he came over to me and extended his hand. "How," he greeted me. "Esscanesh," he said, pointing to his chest. "Your friend. I help you."

I laughed aloud with relief. This Esscanesh had indeed been a friend. "Come inside," I invited him as I shivered in the cold wind. "I'll give you some stew."

Jethro was tossing and turning on the bed with low moans escaping his lips. In a flash Esscanesh was by his side. "Jethro sick?" His voice sounded caring and concerned.

Jethro opened his eyes, which lit up with recognition when he saw the lad. "Esscanesh, help me. I'm dying."

Esscanesh squeezed his shoulder. "No, not die. I go and bring you remedy." Silently he turned on his heels and disappeared out the door. Half an hour later he was back, followed by an old Indian squaw who I think may have been his mother. I knew that these were the friendly Conestogas, who had come with a goodly supply of their Indian remedies! I could have wept for joy as the squaw prepared a mixture over the fire, then going back and forth from the hearth to the bed, administered her potion. She had something for his wounds and something for his fever and pain. She stayed all night to "doctor" him. What a relief it was to hand over my heavy burden to her skilled shoulders. She knows just what to do, even though she doesn't understand more than a few words of our language. I'm thankful that at least Esscanesh can communicate with us.

Tonight I feel more hopeful than I've felt for awhile, but still awfully tired and weak with relief. Esscanesh has left and I'm going to crawl into my bearskin and sleep all night. God has answered my prayers for help and I'm rejoicing and thanking Him constantly.

✍

November 27: Jethro is feeling so much better that Esscanesh and the squaw have gone home, after ministering to him for five days. His fever is down and his wounds are healing. He is very thin, but the way he keeps asking for stew and meat, he should soon regain his strength. This morning I heard a thump at the door, and there was Esscanesh bringing a young buck.

He stayed to help cut up the meat, and we put a goodly portion of it into a stew for Jethro. My trying to thank the Indian lad seems so inadequate. What a blessing he has been to us! If he had not come just when he did, likely our stable and horses would be gone, and with that strong wind, the cabin couldn't have been saved either. And quite likely Jethro would be gone too, for without the squaw's help, could he have gotten better? My heart swells with rejoicing in the knowledge that he is recovering and that we still have sheltering walls and a roof over us. God is good!

✍

November 28: I awoke in the night and heard the stinging of sleet and snow against the cabin walls, and the wind was howling again. A blizzard! I snuggled down deeper into my bearskin and savored the warmth and protection our cabin and the fire on the hearth provided. By morning the drifts were already deep at places, and Jethro fretted about my having to go out into the whirling whiteness. But there was no other way, for he doesn't yet have the strength to do much. I had a hard time wading through the icy mounds to get to the spring. The wind whipped at my shawl and skirts, and stung my face. Back at the cabin, I set the bucket of water inside the door, then headed to the stable to feed the horses. They are always glad to see me—frisking about and nickering joyously. I'm so glad they're still alive! Soon after I was back in the cabin, shivering in front of the fireplace and shaking snow off my shawl, we were frightened by a pounding on the door.

"Let me in!" a deep voice cried. Jethro quickly drew back the bolt and swung open the door. A man, completely covered with snow and ice came stumbling into the room and went straight to the fire. He threw off his icy wraps, then shivering, stood as close to the fire as he dared. "Whew!" he muttered. "It's a genuine nor'easter. I couldn't have gone on much longer. I hope it's all right that I put my horse into your stable."

I noticed that his hair was thick and long, and he had a bushy brown beard. Underneath his shaggy brows, his eyes were blue and twinkly. "Mercy me," he drawled. "I never expected to find a pert young couple in ole' Hendrick's place." There was a wide grin on his face. "Tell me, did you'ns drop right outta the sky?"

I handed him a cup of hot tea, as Jethro and I found ourselves seats near the fire, too, to visit with him. Jethro told him about Uncle Hendrick's fate, as well as all our adventures and misfortunes. When he had finished, the man slapped his knee and laughed a great booming laugh.

"Aren't you young folks the lucky ones now!" he declared. "I just didn't know why the Lord was leading my footsteps in this direction, but now I do. Yes sir, you're in luck. You see, I'm Parson Ames, a traveling minister. If you two want to get hitched, I'm here to perform the ceremony. Then, as soon as the storm blows over, I'll be on my way again. Gotta get over to Neu Strasburg before the week's out, to attend a weddin' there, too. Never thought I'd be killin' two birds with one stone, here."

Jethro spoke up then. "We're not planning to get married . . . now," he said, his voice sounding strained. His face reddened and he glanced at me. "Dorothea Marguerite is on her way to Hans Herr's house. I plan to take her there as soon as my strength returns."

Parson Ames eyed Jethro from head to foot, then said, "By the looks of you, you won't be able to travel for another fortnight. By that time we may be snowed in again, for all you know. Chances are you'll be snowed in until spring. Better take my advice and get hitched now . . . either that, or I'll take the girl along to the Herrs myself. I'm goin' in that general direction. Think it over tonight and let me know in the morning what you've decided. I'm all beat out now, and will feel mighty obliged if you'll let me sack out here in front of your fire."

He soon did just that, and is now snoring so mightily that it nearly shakes the walls. Jethro is pacing back and forth across the room, and every now and then stops to stare at me, then continues his round. He's agitated for sure and I'm certain it's on account of me. He wishes he wouldn't have me on his hands, I'm sure, and doesn't know what to do with me. I'll probably cry myself to sleep again tonight (if such a thing as sleep is possible with the snoring), like I did so often in the weeks after Mother died.

Oh God, take care of me and help me not to be a burden on anyone. Take me home to You, if that is Your will.

✍

"More close calls!" Susie exclaimed. She shuddered to think what might have happened if the Indian lad hadn't come to the poor girl's aid. "And now that traveling preacher is advising them to get married. It sure wonders me what they'll decide. Sixteen is way too young for anyone to get married. Ei yi yi!"

Susie wanted to ask Dannie if they could read for 15 minutes past their usual bedtime, but he was nodding already. *Oh well*, she thought, *tomorrow's another day*. It would never do to oversleep tomorrow morning and be late with the chores. She put away her book and noisily banked the fire, knowing the sound would rouse Dannie.

9

Winter in the Cabin

The next evening Susie quickly washed the milk replacer buckets and stacked them on the rack. She was in a hurry to head back to the house and her book. Would Dorothea Marguerite and Jethro decide to get married? Or, would the parson take her to the Herrs and at some later date the young man would come a'courtin? There was only one way to find out.

🖎

November 29: I finally did fall asleep last night, in spite of the parson's snoring and Jethro's pacing. I was awakened at dawn by someone whispering my name. I sat up at once, and there was Jethro beckoning to me. "We need to talk," he whispered, "now, while the parson's still shaking the cabin with his snoring. Come over here to the table."

(Since I'm living in the wilds of Penn's Woods, I never bother anymore to undress, and so, getting up is a quick thing.) I followed him to the corner, and he quickly (like he wanted to say it before he lost his courage) asked if I'd consider it—our getting married and staying in Uncle Hendrick's cabin until spring. He said he would put out a trapline here with Uncle's traps, and then in the spring he'd carry the furs out. We'd stop at the Herrs and would stay as long as I wished. His proposal nearly took my breath away. I asked for a day to think it over. If it's either that or having to go with the parson, well, I know which I'd choose. But I'm just a little girl, merely 16 and I fear, not at all fit to be a married woman. What answer shall I give him?

The parson tries his best to keep us entertained with stories, but I'm too preoccupied to listen, and I think Jethro is the same.

Oh God, help me to know what to say. It's such a big, life-altering decision. If only my mother were here to give counsel and advice.

✍

December 2: Our little cabin seems awfully quiet with Parson Ames gone, almost too quiet. He left 15 minutes ago, leaving us much parting advice and good wishes.

Jethro sits before the fire, staring into its depth, cupping his chin in his hands. Is he wishing he had decided differently?

My heart is doing flip-flops. Is it maybe all just a dream? Am I really now Mrs. Jethro Arden, or were the parson's words just silly play-acting or pretend? How could I ever have had the courage to say yes—I who am still a child at heart and never had a courtship? I must go to the spring for a bucket of water, and then I'll pay the horses a long visit. The weather has moderated greatly and the snowbanks are disappearing. I must get outside for some fresh air.

✍

December 9: How could I ever have felt the way I did when I wrote my last journal entry a week ago? Jethro is kindness itself and so very good to me. I've never been happier. I feel as if no evil could ever befall me again. No bear could attack me, no Paxton Indians kidnap me, no panther pounce upon me, no sickness waylay me. I am safe and secure. Let the winds roar and the storms howl around our cabin. We are in a cocoon of enchantment that nothing will ever mar.

I remember Anna Herr reminding me that all things work together for good to them that are God's children. When I was being carried off by the Indians, I had no faith that even that could work out for the good. But it did, and Jethro came to my rescue. Time to stir up the fire (but not too much) to get the stew boiling for supper.

✍

December 15: More snow is coming down, gently and silently. I much prefer that kind of snow over the howling blizzard type. Every morning I go with Jethro when he walks his trapline. The snow is beautiful in the woods, especially when the sun glitters on it, setting everything to sparkling. Jethro says he's just about back to where he was before the bear attack, strengthwise that is. We have so much to be thankful for.

I'm working on making a pair of moccasins for myself since my shoes are nearly worn through. I found some deerskin and sinew in the cupboard and have been stitching happily away.

There is so much to learn: doing housewifely things like cooking, sewing, and cleaning. It's cozy here in the cabin, but already I'm looking forward to the warm and lovely spring, and to going to visit the Herrs with Jethro.

✎

December 28: There's time for long talks, after we come in from tramping through the snow. Cozy chats in front of the fire. Jethro has told me of most of his life before we met. He had a good mother and father and it's too bad he lost them at such a young age. But their influence stayed with him and he is living up to their teachings. He tries to obey God as he understands Him, just as I do. There's so much more to learn, which gives me a longing to go back to the Herrs. Both of us were baptized when we were babies, but, according to the Herrs, that's not a believer's baptism upon one's confession of faith. It can't be a symbol of regeneration when an infant is baptized. Maybe someday . . . .

I'll lay this aside for now. Jethro's back, stamping the snow off his feet, and greeting me with his customary "Hello, Little Redhead . . ."

✎

January 5: It's intensely cold out tonight, with the creeks and streams locked under ice and snow. I took a peek outside after dark—all was still and clear, the dark sky studded with brilliant, twinkling stars. Such awesome, aching beauty touched my heart and made me want to cry, for some unexplainable reason.

Jethro was telling me all about the history of Penn's Woods tonight, as we sat in our snug and warm cabin, listening to the howling of the wolves. His store of knowledge astonishes me. Sometimes he talks clear above my head, so I ask him to stop and explain things, and he kindly does. He was telling me more about William Penn, who must've been quite a good man. Penn inherited a vast fortune and used the money to buy these very woods that surround our cabin. Miles and miles of rich soil and vast forests, streams full of fish, and fertile plains. He founded the City of Brotherly Love (Philadelphia). Jethro says that one of Penn's greatest traits was the ability to get along with the Indians. Because of his fairness to them, they loved and respected him. He softened up their wild hearts and thus was able to make a treaty with them. They decided on the "walking purchase plan." For several chests full of trinkets and other goods, the whites were able to purchase a tract of land and then divide it up among the settlers. Two Indians and two white men were to start at a certain point and walk for three days to the west, which would then be the western boundary line of the entire purchase. In other words, the whites' land would be as far east and west as a man could walk in three days. That's why they called it the "walking purchase."

Penn died just a few years ago. I do hope there will be other fair-minded men who are willing to treat the Indians fairly in order to keep peace between us. There is bountiful game in these deep, rich forests, enough for both us and them, if we can co-exist peacefully. I hope the Paxtons are miles and miles away by now and won't return.

✍

February 24: Talking to Jethro about our plans and dreams is not conductive to journal writing, since weeks have passed since my last entry.

There's a new feel in the air. It appears as if winter's grip is receding, and an almost balmy air fills the woods tonight. It's exciting to think of starting off to see the Herrs soon. Jethro is well satisfied with the amount of furs he has taken. Down by the spring tonight, I heard the "kong-a-ree" of a bird that Jethro says are red-winged blackbirds. He says that in a few weeks the robins will be back, too. Soon the wildflowers and herbs will start popping up through the soil. Fact is, I'm glad the winter is nearly over. I loved the warmth and cheer inside our cabin when the icy rains pelted it, and the sleet and snow fell thick and fast. But there's something about spring, that makes you want to skip and rejoice. Jethro's been talking about spring, too. It sort of gets into your bones (or however you would describe the feeling). Springtime is the loveliest time of year!

✍

March 26: Another month is nearly past. Last time I was writing about spring, and here we're having more snow. But it's big, wet flakes floating down and melting as fast as they come. Esscanesh paid us a visit today and brought us a big turkey gobbler. Jethro gave him the royal welcome he so richly deserved! Where would we be if he and the old squaw hadn't helped us out when we needed them? We roasted the turkey for supper, all agreeing it was the most delectable fowl we'd ever tasted. Esscanesh says the Paxtons are nowhere about, that they must've found fairer hunting grounds, which suits me just fine.

I heard a screech owl hooting from the treetops tonight. A few mornings ago, I saw robins hopping about and chirping. I wonder where they keep themselves when it snows?

Jethro just came in the door, saying, "Looky here, Little Redhead. I brought you a bunch of dandelion greens." Hurrah! Spring's here!

✍

April 30: After numerous delays, we're finally starting off on our pilgrimage. I can hardly keep my excitement in hand enough to be as staid and proper as a married woman should be! Penny and Barney were lively and raring to go after their long rest. They're both carrying heaps of beaver, otter, mink, and muskrat furs, so we have to walk.

Surprisingly, after looking forward to our journey for so long, I was almost sorry to leave our little cabin where we were so happy together. Before we left I took a walk down to the little spring (where I chanced to see a raccoon) and felt a twinge of sadness that I wouldn't be fetching buckets of water there anymore. Will we ever come back to it?

I especially loved the almost-sacred Sundays—our quiet sweetness of communing and fellowshipping with The Almighty, and renewing our pledge to walk with the good and wise God, in love and truth. But we shall have our Sundays on the trail, too, and then when we reach the Herrs we will have real worship services!

The lovely birds were flashing and trilling in the woods. We camped tonight under the majesty of the tallest oak tree I ever saw. There was a crimson sunset, and I just sat with my back against a tree, looking about in silent, wondering appreciation. Our fire lit up the firs on the ridge behind us, and high above their fir tops the sky was studded with stars. Jethro says that Penn's Woods are loveliest of all when the dogwoods are blooming, and the ridges are white with trees full of blossoms. It's also very beautiful when the wild phlox patch the slopes with riotous pinks and lavenders. I think they're quite enchanting now. I admire the willows along the creek banks, waving their fresh, light green plumes, and also the heady scent of growing things peeking up through the carpet of last year's leaves. Just now I saw a shy doe bounding away into the thickets, and there's a wolf howling on a faraway hill. I try not to think back to those days when I was alone in the woods and so fearful. I feel much safer when I'm with Jethro, even though I know that the same God was watching over me then as now.

At bedtime Susie closed her book and laid it on the shelf. So now they're married and seem to be happy, she mused. I can't see how they can be, with so many dangers and uncertainties all around them. Perhaps they're immune to them just now, and living one day at a time. That surely would have been the best way, for worrying wouldn't have helped a bit. I wonder what adventures and excitements await them now.

✎

10

A Home in Penn's Woods

On Sunday evening, Susie was finally able to finish the story. She and Dannie had gone for a long walk in the bushland, and paid a visit to Wynn in the trailer. While they were there, Dr. and Mrs. Robinson came in for a friendly chat. Dannie and Dr. Robinson got to reminiscing about the ranch at Horseshoe Knoll, and were talking about spending two weeks there again next summer. Wynn put on a pot of coffee and put out a package of doughnuts for a snack. The conversation was so lively that they quite forgot the time. As a result, Dannie and

Susie were late doing their chores, but Susie was so eager to finish her book that she sat up until 10:30. She felt a bit guilty doing so, but decided it would be okay. *After all*, she rationalized, *in a few years I'll be rumsphringing and probably dating, and then I'll sit up until later than this on Sunday evenings. I might as well start getting used to it now.* She settled back into her rocker and eagerly kept on reading.

✍

May 1: It was another day of traveling with the beauties of springtime all around us. There are rolling, lovely hills in the distance and majestic trees surround us. Sometimes we see wildlife, but silently, like a whisper or a heartbeat, they disappear into hiding. We caught a glimpse of a shy red fox carrying a partridge in its mouth, a deer, some rabbits, and always the joyously singing birds. Tonight, sitting 'round our fire while the horses cropped grass in the clearing, the golden moon shone down through the budding trees, transforming the woods into a shimmering thing of beauty. It was a calm and silent night, but suddenly the peace was shattered by the howling of wolves. They were not close, but I pulled my shawl tightly around me, shivering even though the weather wasn't more than a little bit chilly. Jethro assured me that we were safe. When I am with him FEAR is certainly not the monster it was when I was alone in the woods. We talked about my terror and despair back then, and I wondered, was God displeased that I was afraid instead of trusting Him?

Jethro didn't think so. He said, "God knows our frame, and like a Father pitieth His children, so the Lord pitieth them that fear Him. When a little child is afraid, we do not ridicule it for the fear, we comfort and reassure it."

God does seem close here in the wilderness, even though there are dangers around us. We heaped more wood on the fire to keep the "forest folk" away, knelt to pray, then sought the comfort of our bedrolls.

May 2: It's the time of blooms, blossoms, and birdsongs. The flashy red cardinals sing every morning, and robins sing sweetly all day long. It is a great joy to unexpectedly come across a patch of blooming, shy wildflowers in a hollow, or a patch of fresh watercress in a spring. We saw a flowering bush that was a maze of pink blossoming glory. Some birds are already raising fledglings in their nests. I delight in writing about the woodland beauties, but now I'll write about the danger we encountered today. I can't help but think of it, for it still makes me feel somewhat uneasy.

I was walking along beside Barney, dreamily thinking of the joys of walking through Penn's Woods in May, when Jethro suddenly cried out, in a desperate-sounding voice, "Halt! Stand still!" He grabbed his hatchet and swung it. Twack! There at my feet lay a dead copperhead snake! It was a close call and made me fearfully watch my surroundings the rest of the day. Then tonight, when the stars were peacefully twinkling overhead and the spring peepers chorusing, and I was relaxing into a dozing mood, the forest suddenly rang with the chilling, spine-tingling cry of a fierce panther! We quickly piled more wood on the fire, anxiously waiting to see if there would be a closer one caterwauling. But instead, the next echo of it came from many miles away, and we heaved sighs of relief. The frogs were croaking rhythmically down in the marshes and little creatures were rustling in the thickets, which are relaxing sounds. The woods can be so beautiful and peaceful, but in their sinister depths there are many hidden dangers. I'll be thankful to arrive safely at the Herrs and sleep under a roof, with four solid walls around me. Yet, God is watching over us here outdoors, just as He does in a house.

Time to turn in, so we can make an early start tomorrow morning.

May 10: Our welcome here at the Herr's house was a royal one. Anna is usually an unemotional woman, but when she saw me on her doorstep, she clasped me to her bosom, and we were both blinking away tears. I was so happy to see her!

After supper we visited together on chairs under one of their blossoming apple trees, in the mellow evening sunshine, while Jethro visited with Christian in the blacksmith shop. Grosdaudy Hans joined us there under the tree, too, while the children shyly pressed around us. Elizabeth sat on the grass close beside me, and little Anna crawled up onto my lap. There was so much to tell them of our adventures in the woods. Jethro and Christian joined us later, and together we told them all that had befallen us. I think they, at times, both laughed and cried with us. We shared our plans and dreams with them, and a lengthy discussion ensued.

There is to be a new member in their household in a week or two, and we are planning to stay long enough so that I can be nursemaid to the new little one. Meanwhile, Christian will help Jethro get things together for our journey to a homestead of our own! After my job here is finished, he will loan him the money to rent or buy land west of Hammer Creek. He will also allow him the use of one of his wagons (a covered wagon!) and stock it with all the provisions we need! It is very generous of Christian, and we will work hard to repay him every cent. But best of all is that Grosdaudy Hans and Christian will be giving us more instructions and teachings on the new birth and baptism every evening, preparing us for that important ceremony.

May 15: We had church services here at the Herrs on Sunday. They were very special services for Jethro and I, for we were both baptized. It was a very meaningful and soul-stirring experience for us, both joyous and solemn. As before, Grosdaudy Hans preached the opening message and Christian had the main sermon. It was so reverent and inspiring. I found myself wishing we could find ourselves a homestead close by here, so we could worship here regularly. Faith in God and worshiping Him are so important in facing the stresses and strains in life.

✍

May 16: We are temporarily settled here in the cabin the Herrs vacated when they built the new stone house. There's only a bed, a small table, and two chairs. But, that's all we need for now. The sun shines through the south window making it light and airy inside.

When Jethro is not busy with the preparations for our moving, he helps Christian in the fields. Wouldn't it be nice if we could just stay here! But then we wouldn't have a homestead of our own. Someday we hope to have a family and to support it, we'll need land to plant wheat, rye, flax, hemp, pumpkins, turnips, cabbages, and other garden vegetables. Jethro will clear off the trees and build us a cabin. We'll dream and plan, work, and worship God in this land of opportunity and religious freedom.

✍

May 18: Baby Maria made her appearance at the Herrs this morning, so now I'm busy in the big house. She's a sweet little thing, with a head full of dark hair. Elizabeth and little Anna are so enchanted with her. She's a real live doll to them.

There's churning and baking to do, the garden to hoe, and berries to pick, so I won't waste much time writing. In my spare time I'd rather visit with Grosdaudy Hans, who still freely gives spiritual encouragement and advice when we have a chance to talk. His life has been a full and interesting one, and he has gleaned many spiritual lessons from his experiences.

June 23: Today we started off on our journey to our new home, in Christian's covered wagon, with two strong horses hitched. The Herrs crowded 'round to give us goodbye, as they say it. I couldn't help but shed some tears at the parting, even though we were eager to go. Our spirits were high, yet at the back of our minds were the thoughts of the dangers and hardships that awaited us.

The wagon was loaded with all the provisions we needed, thanks to the Herr's generosity. There was a spinning wheel, bedstead, table, chairs, a walnut chest-of-drawers, and braided rugs. Eight-year-old Christli called out, "Don't let the Paxtons get you!" Anna wiped tears from her cheek and kindly said, "Pay us a visit again, if ever you can." Christian said, "God bless you," and Hans said the same thing in German.

Then we were off, the big wheels creaking'round and'round. The birds were singing joyously and a ring-necked pheasant crowed from a fence row. The horses stepped lively and Jethro had to hold them to a walk, for they had a long way to go.

Both Jethro and I were dreaming golden dreams of excitement, for he said to me, in glowing tones, "Just think, Dorothea Marguerite, soon you'll be cooking on your own hearth, making soap, churning butter, swingling flax and carding wool, and molding candles—nimble-fingered as could be!"

"And you," I retorted laughingly, "will be swinging an ax all day long or plowing a straight furrow in the rich, dark earth; building a cabin, and hunting game. We will carve a homestead out of the wilderness."

"If we live and the Lord wills," Jethro added soberly. "Unless the Lord builds the house, they labor in vain that build it. There will be manifold dangers and trials, I believe. But we will trust in the Lord to be with us."

We rode onward in silence then, with God's peace filling our hearts. There, in the midst of Penn's Woods, was the sure promise, "He will never leave us nor forsake us."

✍

June 24: Twilight is stealing softly and peacefully in the leafy woods as Jethro looks after the horses. Our supper fire is down to a few glowing embers. Tonight we won't need to keep the fire going, for we'll be sleeping in the wagon. So let the wolves howl and the bears prowl! We're camped by a spring which gurgles from among curled fronds of ferns. It flows into a small pool surrounded by a bed of mint. I have to wonder, did some Indian maiden plant that mint there, knowing how fresh, cold and sweet the water tastes after chewing on a sprig of mint?

There's an overflowing thanksgiving in my heart tonight thinking about how we're on our way to a certain tract of land in Penn's Woods, far west of Hammer Creek, where we'll build our own little home—a cabin of sturdy logs to shelter us from the elements and the wild beasts.

Jethro will fell the trees, clear enough land for our garden and crops, and we'll carve a homestead out of the woods. A home of our own at last.

The weather was so beautiful today, clear and cool for June, which may have had something to do with our uplifted spirits. Jethro said he doesn't think the birds have ever sung more sweetly. A pair of redbirds seemed to be following us for a ways, their flashes of scarlet giving us a genuine joy in beholding them. Song sparrows trilled from the bushes, and we saw a meadowlark dipping to its nest in the grass and heard its wistful notes. When we came upon a circlet of wild flowers in sweetly fragrant bloom, I grasped Jethro's arm and urged him to stop the horses for awhile. It was so sweet and beautiful! Jethro pointed out a small, frightened rabbit crouched under the brambles watching us timidly and inquisitively. Delicate green leaves of a trailing grapevine swung gracefully above the brambles, and as we watched, a robin redbreast with a worm in its beak alighted on a branch. Immediately four tiny, wide-open birdie beaks popped out of a nest, and the mother bird fed her young. The woods seemed abundant with new life, filling us with an inward rejoicing. The Creator of all the woodland beauties seemed to be close by in our hushed cathedral, and hand-in-hand we bowed our heads and recited the Lord's Prayer.

The moment was short and sweet for we knew we could not tarry long, and soon the low rumble of the wagon wheels was again our accompaniment. I was utterly weary and longing for rest by the time we made camp tonight, but filled with a satisfying feeling of grateful thanksgiving. Jethro says we've only a few more days of travel and then I can help choose a suitable spot to build our cabin!

A pair of screech owls hooting from the trees startled me a moment ago, but Jethro's reappearance once again bolstered my courage. Sleeping in a wagon seems so much safer than on the ground. Time to lay my quill and copybook aside, for we want to be on our way at the crack of dawn tomorrow. Goodnight.

✍

June 26: I awoke once last night when the moon was high in the sky, and heard a wolf's lonesome howl. It wasn't close but it made me think of all the possible dangers surrounding us. The thoughts of wild animals, hostile Indians, hardships in clearing the land and growing our food, perhaps illness with no doctors to be had, and other fearful things reared their troublesome heads and made me shiver. But peace returned when Jethro awoke and reminded me again of his words as we started off on our journey. He reminded me that God will be with us and of His promise that He will never leave us nor forsake us if we follow His will and trust in Him. So we slept peacefully until the dawning of the morning, when we were again greeted with the joyous singing of the birds. Fears always seem so much worse in the middle of the night than they do when the sun shines and the birds are singing. We happily cooked our breakfast over the fire, then set out once more to find the tract of land which will be our future home.

Our horses were fresh from their night's rest and eager to be on their way, as we wended our way through the dew-covered ferns and bracken, following the barely discernable trail. Once, as we rounded a turn we came upon an animal family. The brown fur-covered mother stood on its hind legs beside a rock, surrounded by its four pudgy babies. At the first sight of us she emitted a piercing whistle blast, and then they all disappeared into a crevice. Jethro said it was a monack family;

an animal that buries itself in its den and sleeps from October until March or April. How curious!

The birds sang sweetly from the towering green trees above us as the morning sunshine filtered through the swaying leaves. I had never really known before how beautiful the woods can be this time of year!

Jethro is as eager to reach our new home as I am, and the horses can hardly travel fast enough to suit him. We chattered nearly as excitedly as the bushy-tailed squirrels in the branches above us, planning and dreaming of our cabin home and of the future until we stopped once more to make camp for our noon meal and to rest the horses. It is good to think that Grosdaudy Hans, Christian, and Anna Herr will be remembering us in their prayers, for where we are going there is no established church yet. We'll gather with the few other settlers of like precious faith on Sunday mornings to sing hymns together and for scripture reading, but there will not be a preacher to expound God's word to us. Hopefully later, when more settlers arrive in the area we will have that, too.

Jethro has in his possession a scroll of hymns which we will practice singing together as we travel through the woods. I'll try to memorize some of the verses, too, and copy some into my journal at times. It is good to keep thoughts of God and His Word in our hearts continually so that our hearts do not become over-charged with the cares of this life. I did already memorize one stanza which I will copy here. Soon I will be too busy for much journal writing, while we are building our cabin.

> *Ye nations round the earth rejoice,*
> *Before the Lord your Sovereign King;*
> *Serve Him with cheerful heart and voice,*
> *With all your tongue His glory sing.*

July 22: I'm sitting on the stone doorstep of our cabin, enjoying the sweetness of a lovely summer evening. All around me in the clearing and amongst the trees are the enchanting flickering lights of flying insects. Jethro says they are called fireflies. When they first appeared, I thought I had never seen anything so lovely and enchanting before! Other night insects are calling too, and frogs are croaking from the banks of the stream. Just a little while ago I was hearing the ringing sound of Jethro's ox reverberating through the woods as he worked at felling trees, but all is silent now and he will be joining me soon.

I will try to write a bit about our arrival at our tract of land and the building of the cabin. There is a shimmering stream flowing nearby, flanked by mighty oaks, elms, and chestnuts, and even a few graceful willows with long green sweeping branches. We stopped by the stream and Jethro got out, lifted up his arms and with an unmistakable note of triumph in his voice, cried, "This is our land—our very own—we paid 17 pounds an acre for it!" He patted the trunk of the huge, spreading tree we were under and said, "Where the trees grow thickest, the land is most productive! Now the making of the homestead is up to us."

Before I could make a reply we heard voices coming through the trees. Very soon a young man and woman appeared and gave us a very hearty welcome to the area. They were Theodore and Sally, our next-door neighbors to the south. Their cabin lies about a mile and a half from us, as they crow flies. They pledged their help in building the cabin, then were soon on their way again.

After we had cooked our noon meal over the fire and were just finished eating, we had another visitor—a long-bearded Swisser in familiar garb. He told us his name is Seth, and that he and his wife Abigail and two children live a mile west of us. He invited us to eat supper with them and spend the night. He said he has seasoned logs and cut lumber we can use for our cabin, which we can then later return to him as Jethro gets time to hew them. How thankful we were for his offers which we gratefully accepted.

After he was gone, we set out to find the best site on which to build the cabin. It had to be near a strong spring, and on enough of a rise to prevent water from coming into our root cellar.

"Here it is!" Jethro cried suddenly as we rounded an immense honeysuckle thicket. There was a touch of awe in his voice as he said, "I won't even need to fell any trees for it. That giant maple will provide shade, and the chopping away of the underbrush won't mean much."

"And here's the spring!" I cried exultantly. "I won't have far to go for water. We can make a rock-lined pool here in which to keep our milk cool."

"I can do better than that," Jethro declared. "I'll build a springhouse for you—sturdy enough to keep the bears and panthers out!"

Hand in hand we returned to our wagon, still planning and dreaming and eager to begin work on the cabin the next day. Our evening at Seth and Abigail's house was wonderful, too. Abbie, as she said we can call her, is a cheerful, bustling, motherly type of person, and Seth is as helpful and friendly as one could wish. Their little Hannes and Mary are as sweet as Christian and Anna Herr's children. How thankful I am that we have good neighbors close by!

Ya well, writing about our cabin must wait until next time, for Jethro is coming up the path. By the time he comes in, he is so tired from swinging his ax all day that sitting up to visit awhile is out of the question. How good the straw tick and featherbed feel to tired and aching muscles and bones.

✍

July 27: I'm sitting by the murmuring stream, in the shade of a huge elm, cooling my feet in the soothing water while I rest my back, weary from gardening. The late vegetable crops are doing well, and the rainfall has been adequate. While I rest I'll write about the raising of our cabin.

Seth and Abbie, and Theodore and Sally came over bright and early as had been planned on that first day we started putting up the cabin. Rafter poles were set, rib poles placed, cracks were filled with clay clinking, and stout widths of hickory logs were lashed into position. I was amazed at how soon the small two-room cabin took shape against the background of trees.

The inside work took awhile. Building the huge fireplace out of native limestone and putting up the crane and kettles were tiresome. After it was all finished, I set up my spinning wheel and laid down the braided rugs Anna Herr made and gave to us. We have two small windows with real glass in them which Seth brought from Hickorytown. Our table, two side chairs, chest-of-drawers, and bedstead will have to suffice for now, but as he gets time, Jethro will make us more furniture. I dearly prize the sewing basket Anna Herr gave to me with its precious pins, needles, thread, and scissors, and also the medicine chest containing dried hoarhound, Golden Remedy, and sage tea. Abbie will teach me to boil soap, churn butter, and preserve vegetables and fruit. She gave me a lovely gift—a patchwork quilt in star design! It's not new, but it's pretty, and brightens up our little bedroom. How will I ever repay all the kindnesses done to me?

It's "Home Sweet Home," our dear cozy little cabin, and we can hardly thank enough the Giver of all good gifts, for all these blessings. Only one thing is lacking yet, and that is a cradle and a dear little bundle to lay into it. Lord willing, someday that will be our portion, too. I've memorized another verse of a hymn which I'll copy here before I lay this aside.

O draw me, Saviour, after Thee!
So shall I run and never tire.
With gracious words still comfort me;
Be Thou my hope, my solemn desire.
Free me from every weight: nor fear
Nor sin can come if Thou are here.

August 12: Our barn and fence are finished now, too, and Jethro came home tonight riding a fine bay stallion. He was smiling broadly as he rode up to me where I was pulling weeds in the turnip patch, and dropped a squirming sack at my feet. I heard a whine, and the next moment a furry head burst out! It was a cute puppy all cuddly and lovable.

"A pet for you," Jethro said. "He should make a fine watch dog later. I got both the horse and pup from a trader."

My heart thrilled at the sight of it for, though I am busy from dawn 'til dusk, my heart feels lonely while Jethro is clearing his fields all day. I cherish our meal times together, but when the loneliness becomes overwhelming, I join Jethro in the woods. I take along my sewing and find a fallen log or suitable rock to sit on and work. Also, twice I have gone through the woods to Abbie's, and once to neighbor Sally. It will cheer my heart to have a puppy following at my heels. We put the horse into his corral and he stood looking friendly-like at us over the fence, before he went off to graze. Jethro named him Star, after a horse he had before he came to the New World. We will keep the pup in the cabin, for he is too small to defend himself against wild varmints. I shall call him Marquis, after the friendly young man who befriended me on the ship coming over—Hannah Keith's son. I'll never be able to forget the hardships we endured on the journey across the ocean.

Neighbor Abbie told me that they too had a perilous time on the ship coming over. Many died, including her 7-year-old sister. Her 13-year-old brother was very sick with scurvy. His eyes were sunken, his cheeks sallow, and his lips swollen. He kept begging for a red apple. I guess his body knew what it needed and caused the craving. He also asked for potatoes and cabbage, but there were none to be had. To distract him, his mother reminded him of the brethren, how they were persecuted, driven from their homes, and burned at the stakes without mercy. But still his pleading continued, mostly for a red, red apple. The captain came to see him, and seeing that death was close, said grimly, "He knows what he needs, but apples don't grow in the ocean." The boy survived though until they reached land, and someone quickly supplied them with apples. By that time he was almost comatose, but they scraped the pulp of the apple and put it between his lips. He swallowed it down and begged for more. Soon he was wide awake and eating a scraped potato also. When they asked him how he feels, he said, "I feel as if I'm going to be able to see Penn's Woods after all." He is now hale and hearty again, but it was a close call.

Time to set the bread, and then to scrub the cabin floor. The puppy lies curled on a bed of pines near the hearth, sleeping contentedly. Peace and plenty, home and hearth.

August 23: I had quite a scare this morning. It was all I could do to quench a scream! I was ladling mush out of the kettle when a shadow fell across the open door. I whirled around and there was an Indian! I was so startled that I nearly dropped the ladle! But with a smile he raised a hand in greeting and then I recognized him. Esscanesh!

Jethro came in just then and gave him the welcome he deserved. They had a good visit while he ate with us, and then he was soon ready to be on his way again. His parting words were, "While the sun shines and water flows we are friends." Their people hunt the deer and bear in the forests and fish in the streams and rivers. The squaws make clothes from animal skins and huts of bark. Jethro says that as long as we keep the treaty William Penn made with them, and treat them fairly, Esscanesh's people will not make trouble for us. My heart rejoices at the end of each day of peace and safety, and may it always remain so.

The woods are peaceful and hushed tonight as I sit on the stone doorstep. All summer I listened to the cheerful trilling of the birds, and picked the wildflowers by the stream with which to brighten my kitchen. Now there are signs of the approaching autumn, when the leaves will change to bright hues and then wither away. Our days have been work-filled and weary, and sometimes too lonely, but mostly we have been happy here together in our tranquil spot. Jethro says that someday we will have a sturdy stone house and many more acres cleared and I know that he is thinking too, of the sturdy sons and daughters we hope to have. When we kneel to pray at bedtime, I never forget my secret prayer asking the great God of the universe to grant us our wish.

September 3: Abbie and Seth and little Hannes and Mary were here yesterday for a very welcome visit. They brought along a basket of apples—oh how sweet they tasted! As we visited, Abbie and I peeled apples for drying, and I couldn't keep from popping a slice into my mouth time and again. I had to think of Abbie's brother who nearly died from lack of fruits and vegetables in his diet, and I felt very thankful for the privilege.

While Hannes and Mary played in the corner, Abbie told me of the harrowing experience they had the last time they drove to Hickorytown. On the way home, in a lonely stretch of the dark woods, a rough-looking man suddenly stepped out trying to blocking their way. They shook with fear when they saw the gleam of a rifle barrel as he barked out an order for them to hand over their money and goods. Their big mongrel dog had gone along and was walking under the wagon as he usually did, being smart enough to keep away from the wheels. He crept out from under the wagon and circled the man, then with a mighty bark, leapt onto him from behind, knocking the man to his knees. The impact knocked the rifle from his hand and he clutched at his throat as he cried, "Help! Call him off! He'll be at my throat!" Seth instructed the dog to hold the man, then leapt from the wagon, grabbed the rifle and unloaded it and threw it as far into the woods as he could. They quickly rode away while the dog guarded the robber. Not until they were at home did the dog reappear. It makes me uneasy thinking about such unsavory characters round about. I hope none come our way, ever. Jethro says that such bandits stay near the towns, and I hope that he is right.

Abbie and I had so much to talk about, for if day after day passes by without another woman to talk to, my heart feels starved for feminine conversation. She is so blessed to have her little boy and girl to care for.

Jethro and I sat on the stoop to visit and reminisce awhile after they left. We are going to help Abbie and Seth boil applebutter next month, and they have promised us several crocks of it for our winter's use. My mouth waters for it already. Jethro says that I am the best bread baker in all the New World, but fresh applebutter will make it taste so much better.

It's time to lay this aside now and make a pot of tea for us before it's time to crawl into the straw tick. The feather bed on top makes it very comfortable for weary muscles and aching bones. Goodnight.

✍

October 12: Some new settlers have moved in two miles southwest of us, and built a small cabin. Jethro says that the proprietors are so anxious to have the land cleared and settled that they look the other way when squatters move in on unoccupied land grants. The quitrent, which is usually a halfpenny an acre, is seldom collected. The newcomers don't seem to want to be very friendly or sociable, but perhaps we'll be able to befriend them somehow.

I went for a walk in the woods today with Marquis the pup following at my heels. We heard chestnuts and acorns thud as squirrels and chipmunks rustled through the dry leaves, scampering here and there as they foraged for nuts to add to their stores. Flamboyant crimson maples and golden sassafrass blazed with glory. Virginia creepers poured like red wine over a fallen log, and at the edge of a clearing the brown sedge and goldenrod flaunted their gay color alongside the flaming sumac. Autumn is here in all its beauty and glory, and next will be the cold, snowy winter. How thankful we are for a plenteous harvest and bountiful provisions.

Jethro isn't quite so busy anymore now that the crops are in, and we have more time to spend together. My favorite time is in the evening when we sit before the fire watching the dancing flames and dreaming enchanting dreams, planning and hoping, and sometimes just sitting in contented silence. Outside, the wolves howl on faraway hillsides, and the chilly wind whips around the chimney. I've memorized another verse of a hymn which I will copy here.

The light of truth to us display,
And make us know and choose Thy way;
Plant holy fear in every heart,
That we from God may ne'er depart.

✍

November 28: I sit here in fear and tremble as the wind shrieks and rattles around the trembling cabin walls, and as hard bits of snow and sleet are flung against the windows. My heart has been afraid for so long—it's been two days since Jethro has gone off into the woods with his gun, trailing the big bear that had been nosing around our stable. I try not to think of what could have happened to him. I dare not allow myself to think of it. But there are so many dangers in the woods and now this unrelenting blizzard yet, too. I've been praying without ceasing, trying to trust and believe, but that monster Fear keeps coming back. Oh, Jethro, how very much I still need you. I dare not allow myself to start crying, for fear I'd not be able to stop! To distract myself, I'm trying to read the book that Abbie loaned to me. It was written by a man named John Bunyan who spent 12 years in prison because he would not stop preaching. Twelve years away from his wife and children! In the book, the man Christian, searches for the Celestial City which represents our journey of life with its temptations and problems. But it's no use trying to read, for I can't concentrate when the Fear monster keeps attacking me. I keep telling myself that Jethro will soon be at the door, home safe at last, and all will be well. O God, watch over him and keep him safe.

✍

November 29: I was exhausted and fell asleep on the rug near the hearth last night. Suddenly I was awakened by a noise at the door—a stamping of feet and muffled thumps. I had been dreaming and when I opened my eyes, I saw that my dream had come true! Jethro was standing by the door, trying to shed his frozen snow-covered wraps. With a cry of joy I ran to help him. He was half frozen, but home safe at last. I piled more wood on the fire, and soon had the pot of stew reheated, for he was half-starved as well as nearly frozen. It went awhile until he was even thawed enough to talk, and then he told me all about his experiences. He had trailed the bear for a day, and then had to turn back because the snowstorm was coming. He very nearly lost his way entirely. It was only by the grace of God that he made it.

We've had a quiet day together today, almost too awed and shakened to talk. Life is so rare and precious, and so uncertain. The tears just insisted on filling my eyes. Tonight I told Jethro what I had been suspecting for a week or two already, for I believe that he will need to make a cradle. If my calculations are correct, we'll be needing it in early June. He was jubilant, but I was still too shaken from my fears for Jethro, and the uncertainties and dangers of life to rejoice with him. I know I shall be feeling better soon, and as delighted as he is, but for now, the tears keep filling my eyes. The hardships of pioneer life—wild beasts, bandits, possibly savage Indians, no available doctor— all together it seems overwhelming. I pray for the help and strength I need.

I have only one sheet left in my copybook, and so I won't even have the solace of journal writing anymore. But Jethro has reminded me of "My Grace Is Sufficient For Thee," and I want to lean on that promise. I think I'll save the last page for writing about the little one when it arrives. I'll pray daily that all will be well.

✍

June: A robin sings sweetly from the big tree behind our cabin, and a fragrant evening breeze drifts in through the window. I can hear the sound of Jethro singing in the stable, and my heart answers with a song of its own. Little Christian stirs in his cradle, and my heart stirs with motherly love. He is such a sweet little bundle and healthy, too. Abbie was here for the birth and the first day, and she was as good as a doctor would have been. How full is my heart of praise and thanksgiving!

I've memorized more verses and I'll fill my last page with one and say goodbye to journal writing, for I have no more paper or copybook.

> *Awake, my love! Awake my joy!*
> *Awake, my heart and tongue!*
> *Sleep not when mercies loudly call;*
> *Break forth into a song.*
> *This day God was my sun and shield,*
> *My Keeper and my Guide;*
> *His care was on my frailty shown,*
> *His mercies multiplied.*

By the time Susie had reached the end, her eyelids were drooping. She quickly locked the doors and headed up the stairs. Dannie had already banked the fire and gone to his room. *The story ends rather abruptly,* she mused, as she crawled between the blankets. *I wish it could have continued. I would have liked to read more about their life in the woods and about the homestead they carved out of the wilderness.* On the last page of the journal a bit of information had been added about the couple, but not enough to satisfy one's curiosity. It said that Jethro and Dorothea Marguerite had 9 children, 4 of whom lived to be only a few years old. Dorothea Marguerite died at the age of 39, leaving 5 young children. Jethro lived to be 48 years old. *In all probability they had their share of trials, hardships, and dangers*, Susie thought, as she drifted off to sleep. *Lots of sadness, too, when their children died.*

On Monday morning Dannie and Susie were surprised and overjoyed to see a van come heading in the lane. "It's Steven, Annie, and Suzanne!" Susie cried, jumping up and down and clapping her hands. "They're here sooner than we thought!"

It was a joyous homecoming. Steven was well pleased with how Dannie had taken care of things in the barn, and Annie was pleased to see that Susie had the house looking as spotless as always. "Be it ever so humble," she said, looking around her dear, familiar kitchen, "there's no place like home. The best part of traveling is always coming home!"

On Tuesday Susie received a letter from Nancy and Andrew. They had sent a prompt reply by return mail, with some information about the Hans Herr House they had visited in the fall. Nancy wrote:

Hans and Christian Herr were among the first of their people to come to the New World. They settled on a tract of land in Penn's Woods. A surveyor for the colony called them the "long-bearded Switzers." (They came from Germany, but were originally from Switzerland.) More and more immigrants soon arrived, and within a few years the new settlement was a bustling community. There were not only farmers, but also a miller, a bricklayer, a blacksmith, two physicians, weavers, house carpenters, and several land agents. By 1719 when the Herr's new stone house was built, the settlement had grown from 7 families to more than 66. The farmers quickly adapted to their new environment and started to grow wheat, rye, hemp, flax, and of course, plenty of garden vegetables. In less than a decade, the new settlement became known for its abundance of produce. Penn's Woods were fertile and had adequate rainfall.

Hans Herr died in 1725, at the age of 86, according to genealogy records.

In 1969 the Lancaster Mennonite Historical Society was able to purchase the old Hans Herr House and the surrounding acreage. They restored the old house to its original 1719 appearance, and since 1975, it has been a museum for the public. An orchard of historic apple varieties was planted to demonstrate the importance of apple growing to the early pioneers. Two barns are exhibit areas for old tools and implements. A blacksmith shop and an outdoor bake oven were also reconstructed. They often have special events to demonstrate the making of colonial and rural crafts, the use of farm tools, and to sell homemade foods. They have Snitz Fests and Candlelight evening programs available by special arrangements. It would be interesting to attend these events to learn more about how the early pioneers in Penn's Woods lived.

✍

Susie folded the letter and put it back into the envelope. *Perhaps someday I'll go and see it, too,* she was thinking. *It would be so interesting, picturing Anna Herr busy cooking over the hearth in the küche, and Christian plowing the fields surrounding the house, Grosdaudy Hans would be on the rocker beside the stove, reading his bible, and the children would be studying their lessons around the table, or outside playing.*

She could imagine the Sunday services in the *stube,* their German singing echoing from the ceiling, and Christian's ringing voice expounding the scriptures.

Next she pictured another scene: The rooms filled with the rank odor of bear grease when 30 Indians packed into it to get out of the storm, as Nancy had added in a postscript to her letter.

A sweeter picture was that of pretty, dark-haired baby Maria in the cradle, and Anna Herr picking her up, then humming softly and rocking her to sleep.

Susie resolved, "As soon as I get home to our Whispering Brook Farm in Pennsylvania, I'll ask Mom and Dad to take us over to see the Hans Herr House. Finding out more about our forefathers and other pioneers and how they stood for the right can be very beneficial." She began to hum the song, *Faith of our Fathers, living still, in spite of dungeon, fire and sword . . . Faith of our Fathers, holy faith, we will be true to Thee 'til death.*